Also by Philippe Djian

Consequences

a novel

Philippe Djian

Translated from the French by Bruce Benderson

Simon & Schuster Paperbacks
New York   London   Toronto   Sydney   New Delhi

Simon & Schuster Paperbacks
A Division of Simon & Schuster, Inc.
1230 Avenue of the Americas
New York, NY 10020

First Simon & Schuster trade paperback edition September 2013.
Originally published in French in 2010 by Éditions Gallimard.

For information about special discounts for bulk purchases, please contact Simon & Schuster Special Sales at 1-866-506-1949 or business@simonandschuster.com.

The Simon & Schuster Speakers Bureau can bring authors to your live event. For more information or to book an event, contact the Simon & Schuster Speakers Bureau at 1-866-248-3049 or visit our website at www.simonspeakers.com.

Manufactured in the United States of America

10 9 8 7 6 5 4 3 2 1

Library of Congress Cataloging-in-Publication Data is available.

ISBN 978-1-4516-0759-8
ISBN 978-1-4516-0760-4 (ebook)

Consequences

*I*f there was one thing he could still do at fifty-three in a vast winter night bleached by the moon—after three bottles of very strong Chilean wine—it was take the coast road with his foot to the floor.

He was driving a Fiat 500—motor on the way out—but more than powerful enough to heave him to the bottom of the cliff, if he didn't keep a firm hand on the wheel and eyes open on the road.

Freezing air gushed through the window. The tires screeched on cue at every hairpin curve. Over the years, a lot of idiots had been killed on this road, but that didn't stop him from braving it.

He'd never been able to bring himself to stay in town, no matter what he'd done or drunk or taken—never. No one had ever been able to keep him from getting into his car and driving home. Not on this road. Not this goddamned road, in any case.

There was a young woman with him, and she seemed tipsy, too. He glanced at her, marveling again that an old prof in a sports jacket, with such a small car, was still lucky enough to attract a student—and take her back to his lair for one full night of fun, at least.

Quite a few years ago, he'd understood that the time had come to take advantage of certain perks that came with his profession—for lack of the better rewards that he had to stop expecting. One day, by a kind of miracle, one of his students began to glow as he looked at her—from the inside out, like a Chinese lantern with a wonderful gleam—but was, despite this, insipid and ordinary, almost devoid of interest, and absolutely incapable of putting two sentences together. Yet, just as he was brutally jeering, in front of the other students, at work she'd turned in, he was blinded by a blast of heat. And this girl turned out to be the first in a fairly long series, as well as one of the most satisfying lays he'd ever had.

When it came down to it, serial relationships with young students were far from fruitless ordeals. There were guys blowing themselves up in the middle of crowds for a lot less than that.

The one with him tonight, whose name escaped him, had just signed up for his writing class, and he hadn't for a second fought his outrageously strong attraction to her. Why should he? It was promising to be a chilly, lazy weekend, perfect for the fireplace. And for sulky mouths, and the deepness of thighs. He only hoped she'd be ready for it when the time came.

Had she passed out? The seat belt kept her from collapsing to either side. He'd need to make some coffee when they arrived.

The shoulders of the road were white, the undergrowth inky black. Jaw clenched, he held to the center of the road, straddled the white line that twisted under his eyes like a hungry snake in an April moon.

_____

She was twenty-three. At dawn, he noticed she was dead, cold.

He was dumbfounded for a moment; then threw off the sheets, bounded out of bed, and glued his ear to the door. The house was quiet. He listened carefully, before turning back to the bed to study the girl's body. At least there was no blood. A stroke of luck. Under the strong light flooding the room, she seemed absolutely pristine, smooth, milky.

He wouldn't wait any longer and got dressed, remembering how he'd almost had to carry her from the car to the bed—about as full of life as a sack of apples and about to be sick any second. Then, suddenly, when they reached the bedroom, she came to. Was thrilled to be there, at his place—*finally* there. Ripped off her clothes, sending her panties sailing across the room. He had no idea what happened next but was sure of one thing—they'd done it. They had.

Every one of these girls was more incredible than the last— and this one, whom you might call a beauty, despite somewhat short legs, hadn't broken the rule. Even in this condition, terribly dead and getting colder and colder, she was still a knockout. He lowered his eyes.

Future problems stood out. Big problems. And nothing would bring the poor girl back to life, not in any way at all. Nothing more could be done for her.

The sun was rising. Treetops glistened. A thick carpet of snow covered the ground. At the moment, getting rid of her body seemed the most realistic thing to do. Who wanted to get mixed up with the police in this country? Who still believed being innocent meant you'd be left in peace? He opened the window.

Not a sound coming from the nearby woods. Crows traced circles in the sky; buzzards on the hunt glided in slow-motion. Below them, the lake emerged from shadow, became a mirror on which the first paddle boats—fledged like arrows—were already gliding. His bathrobed sister appeared in the garden for her first cigarette of the day. She looked up at him.

"Hi, Marianne." He waved. "Nice day, huh?"

"Marc. For God's sake. You made such a racket last night."

"You talking about my muffler?"

"There was somebody with you."

"With me? No, you were dreaming. Must have been the TV."

A block of snow slid from the roof and landed with the smothered sound of heavy meringue. He shrugged and moved away from the window. They were still a couple of weeks from spring, but for a moment he thought he'd detected a subtle perfume in the air—first flowers that had opened during the night—but maybe he hadn't. He couldn't smell anything now. The ice and snow had closed back over them.

The girl was as cold as a ham, nearly gray already. He took a deep breath, began to collect the poor thing's possessions.

Then he began to dress her, thinking for a second about holding on to the white cotton panties, which released a faint odor of urine. He readjusted the brassiere that she hadn't taken off, slipped on her stockings. Now he could picture a few scenes from the evening before as they were heading for the cottage, each as drunk, as out of it, as the other, both mostly unaware that they were.

The sun had begun to lap the other bank; the forests were emerging from darkness in blazing strips. The student's body had been entirely waxed. How sad to see her stretched out like that; stiff and useless, shifted forever into another world. After the time she'd given him.

The beginnings of an erection awarded his work, such thoughts. But there were too many things on the calendar today, and he pushed the young woman's legs closed. He'd just heard the coffee machine downstairs. The way would be free in about ten minutes. He'd take advantage of that time to swallow a handful of aspirin, before his skull threatened to explode.

He checked that he wasn't forgetting anything: keys, phone, cards, cash, briefcase, hat, trifocals, then threw his dismal load over one shoulder and walked down with it on tiptoe.

He was lucky he was still in pretty good shape for his age, because she must have weighed about 130 and wasn't exactly helping—especially on the stairs, where you had to be careful not to miss a step.

Crossing through the kitchen, he grabbed an apple for breakfast. Outside, the sun was shining; snow crunched and pulverized like sugar under his feet. It was a nice day, cold. He leaned the girl against the car door and set about hacking the Fiat out of its ice shell with a scraper he'd gotten from Total. He tried to put his mind on his class, the talk on John Gardner he was planning to give—even if they accused him of being a fanatical ultra-Americanist and betrayer of French literature.

Who were the real traitors? Who was hiding the truth? The difficulties began when he had to get the young woman into the car. The legs were the problem. There was so little room. He had to push hard. Bend her bones. Any second now and Marianne could come back and ask what he was up to. What would he say? At any moment, neighbors might go by on the road, or joggers, who'd stop and ask questions.

By not giving up, by bracing himself and putting his back into it, he made something give way—he refused to dwell on what—and the student was finally inside the Fiat. He glanced at his watch; time to get going. He gave two little beeps of the horn as he started out—one of those pathetic customs Marianne and he had established over the course of time, which both of them regretted equally but endured even though his sister hadn't appeared at the window for ages and he'd stopped even glancing into his rearview mirror.

For several days he'd been wondering whether he hadn't lost part of his muffler—the whole thing, in fact. Certainly, the Fiat 500 had never been much when it came to discretion—he'd given up on buying an Audi A8 someday despite everything. But right now you'd have said a tractor, a motorcycle with no muffler, or a jet plane was taking off nearby. He'd have to do something, find a solution. Lately, in town, they were beginning to look up as he drove by; it wouldn't be long before they had him in their sights for it and nabbed him, maybe even handcuffing him and taking him to the police station with a gun pointed to his temple. A couple of days ago, a professor from the English department had been tackled to the ground and beat up in plain view for a couple of points on his license; and, nowadays, even Human Rights Watch made no stink about such details—nobody paid it much attention anymore. If not that, then sooner or later Marianne was going to make it her business to let him know she'd had it up to here with his nocturnal outings. You could count on that. She wouldn't stand for it much longer—unless he got himself a bike and greased the chain regularly.

Halfway to the campus, he parked on the shoulder behind

a stand of snow-covered trees. The air felt harsh, raw; every breath sent a white stream of vapor swirling in the sunlight. He took his time rolling up his cuffs. His cheeks were red already. He couldn't say as much for his passenger's. Before taking care of her, he checked his messages. Verified that a part of the world hadn't been razed in the night or infested by a virus; there was certainly nothing about it in the papers. Cold, dry, pleasant weather was on the menu. The usual atrocities happening here and there.

He gave it a nod of approval and mentally prepared himself for the climb. The path was steep and narrow, hardly negotiable, and certain parts of it were downright acrobatic. He'd get to the top breathless and drowning in icy sweat, and show up in front of his students a little more rumpled and slovenly than he would have wanted—but fate was deciding otherwise, and every man had to submit to it.

The student had turned bluish gray—not that it was really that cold. *What a shame*, he thought. He felt a pang of anguish as he bent over her and grabbed her under the arm. What a tragedy, when you thought about it. Kicking the bucket at such a young age. How absurd, sickening. And what a nasty trick to play on him, too. What a very dirty trick to play on him, making that poor girl give up the ghost right under his roof, in his bed. Why hadn't they put a knife in his hand, for good measure? Boy, was this rough. Grimacing, he hoisted her to his shoulders.

He and Marianne had once discovered this pit by accident, on a day when he'd just missed suddenly sliding into it. He'd stayed there hanging above a void, a deep hole that gaped into a steep, moss-covered slope, hidden from sight. He owed his life entirely to his sister, who'd grabbed hold of him and yanked him up with all her might. When they'd gotten their breath back and shakily returned to the hole, they saw that its open jaws, which were level with the ground, were wide enough to swallow a horse or a cow.

Very quickly, icy sweat began trickling between his shoulder blades. It was obvious he smoked too much. He was going to have to face that problem squarely; no longer any doubt about it. His lungs were on fire. So were his calves. A few years more of this routine and his tongue would be hanging out, his knees scraping the ground.

Nevertheless, the first thing he did after shoving the young woman's body over the edge—keeping his ears needlessly pricked—was to light one up. His Winstons were on his team one hundred percent. Add fresh air scented with snow-covered grass, and you almost had bliss: he could testify to it. Half smiling, he studied the reddening tip. Right now, the silence around him was so profound that he could hear the faint crackle of the tobacco burning. You could hardly believe the silence of these vibrant winter woods covering the surrounding mountains.

No matter how many times he wore his good Galibier walking shoes, his socks always got drenched, and so were the bottoms of his trousers, which had changed from light beige to dark brown. What's more, he'd gotten pretty dirty during the climb. He'd slipped twice on sheets of ice, and had to force his way through a difficult passage between blocks of stone and low branches while still weighted down by his burden. There wasn't enough time to go home and change. How stupid of him. He should have realized he wouldn't be able to clamber all the way up with that girl on his shoulder and come back down fresh as a lily. (A memory of himself as barely a teenager, in shorts, covered with dust and dried mud passed fleetingly through his mind.) He and Marianne. Ushered directly to the bathtub. Manhandled under the shower by that horrible woman.

*B*arbara. *He'd remembered her first name two days later,* when things started to develop. Barbara. That perfectly stupid name he'd hurried to forget, since it didn't do justice to the girl who hadn't taken long in class to reveal quite a few talents, and whose writing wasn't half bad. He'd spotted her immediately. Blond and shy, well-behaved—that was the type— but with a heart burning like a handful of hot coals. He got up and looked out his office window. He was moved by her memory. Rare were students you could get any work out of, students with promise. During all these years, he'd seen so many of them go by, but he could count on the fingers of one hand the ones who'd be able to produce solid work. You needed a minimum of a gift for it. Either you had it or you didn't. And he didn't. He'd ended up a hair's breadth from terra firma, a millimeter short of the other shore. But without a smidgen of the gift to start with, insisting was useless. Such was always the subject of his first lecture at the beginning of the year, when he cautioned them against too much optimism or self-confidence, based on the number of elect among the new arrivals. Even second fiddles were rare. Even good screenplay writers. In about fifteen years, he'd only come across two or three of the truly talented, just two or three who'd brought a touch of brilliance to his classes. Tiny drops in the bucket. Such rarity was staggering—it made you humble when you taught writing and fell upon a gem.

His eyes followed the detective, who'd left his card and was now walking across the parking lot reserved for tenured professors and the disabled. The temptation had been strong for a brief moment; he'd been tempted to tell the truth, admit that they'd left the party together and ended up in his bed. But he'd come to his senses in time. The truth alone wouldn't have done anyone any good.

The trees were beginning to bud. The detective made a noisy, jittery half-turn in the parking lot and drove back across the campus at fifty an hour. Not that he'd been disturbed by their talk. On the contrary, they'd hit it off; but then the detective had gotten a message on his radio about a ram-raiding car smashing into the window of a jewelry store a few minutes from the city center, and taking millions of euros with it.

What a fascinating profession. The arrival of spring obviously made such work even more fun—you drove with one elbow resting on your open window, could stop to have a drink without owing anybody an explanation, could even tail pretty ladies, eat lunch with all expenses paid, carry a gun, etc., as the detective had explained. A profession all about adventure in the open air.

At any rate, nobody had seen the famous Barbara and him leaving together that night. It was a basic precaution he'd always taken, from the time he'd begun having these kinds of relations. Sleeping with a student was still very badly perceived; more often than not, you were gambling with your job if you ended up before the disciplinary committee. Usually, he broke it off before complications intervened, before they were caught in flagrante delicto, before his safety measures started getting sloppy. He was used to it here, had no desire to put his job in danger for what he saw as recreation, fringe benefits.

The sky was ablaze. He pulled together his belongings, shoved a bundle of papers under his arm, and headed for the exit as the sun was nearing its zenith. He gulped down a sandwich in the cafeteria, because Marianne probably hadn't bothered to make them a pot-au-feu. At times—right now, for example—Marianne lived exclusively on cottage cheese, fat content, zero percent. He couldn't explain why any more than she could but that wasn't very important.

Barbara's death had clearly curbed his appetite, but this morning he was feeling better. The self-control and composure he'd given proof of in front of the detective—his perfect performance—deserved some reward, even if the ordeal hadn't been very difficult to endure on his territory, behind his professor's desk, which automatically put the detective at a disadvantage.

He dug up some coins and walked to the coffee machine. Lit a cigarette. It wouldn't be his first fine for smoking in a public place; there was nothing he could do about it. He'd been poisoned by one of the strongest drugs, which caused the most powerful dependency. These people now under attack—the cigarette manufacturers—were agents of evil, authentic assholes, but pure geniuses, too, fantastic chemists.

While the machine ground his coffee and then released a cup and stirrer that looked like an ice cream stick, he turned his back to the room to watch the gulls flying over the lake. Then a hand grazed his shoulder.

It was truly rare to be able to finish a smoke without a

twenty-year-old girl rolling horrified eyes and remarking that she refused to come down with throat cancer because of him. Sighing and smiling faintly, he turned around, fully aware that he wasn't setting a good example yet bathed from head to toe in his cherished nicotine. Before him stood a fairly attractive woman, close to fifty. An unusual occurrence for this campus, but certainly a pleasure—sooner or later too many smooth faces caused an overdose.

"I'm Barbara's mother," she said.

"Oh, sorry. Nice to meet you," he answered, quickly extending a hand.

Few students could resist the temptation to confide in their moms—even if he asked them from the start to hold their tongues. For the most part, keeping a secret seemed well beyond their feeble powers. Once a mother had thrown her drink in his face as he was lunching peacefully at the pier. Any threats he'd come close to were from that sphere alone. So he put his guard up straight away.

Touching his arm, she said, "Can we sit down? May I speak to you?"

He raised his eyes for an instant, took her in. Even though there weren't many people around, she led him to the table farthest away. Outside, a cold wind was blowing; but behind these plate glass windows it was hot. "I don't want to bother you," she said.

"Not at all. Not in the slightest. What are you having?"

They ordered coffee. "You're her teacher. She'd talk about you."

He tried to interpret the look in her eyes. What was she after? What did she know? He tried to read her mind, and couldn't; but in the process noticed what a graceful oval her chin formed. Amazing how women today managed to keep themselves in shape—Sharon Stone, for example.

"Talk to me about her. About my daughter. Barbara."

"Talk to you about what?"

"Yes, talk to me about her, please."

Later, as he was heading home, driving sensibly—smiling at radar traps and faintly nodding at two frisky motorcycle cops as he let them pass—he went over his conversation with Barbara's mother. The poor woman was worried sick, wondering if there'd been some kind of accident.

He'd tried to reassure her, but without insisting too much or giving her too much hope. Unfortunately, you always had to prepare yourself for the worst, he'd murmured, as his hand encircled her wrist—a very shapely, very white one. "I'm pleased with her," he'd hastened to add. "Thrilled to get this chance to tell you so. Very pleased with her. I expect a lot more from her."

Was that all he could have said? Halfway home, he stopped and parked behind the still-frozen slope and inspected the area around the path he'd taken two days before with Barbara's body over his shoulder. He frowned a little as he recalled the image. *But when fate has you in its grip*, he thought, *what good does it do to resist?*

It wasn't quite as cold as the last time. He could feel spring arriving at full gallop, spot a few snowdrop blossoms here and there.

"Tell you what?" he'd replied. "You must know her better than I do. Hah . . . hah, aren't I right?" he'd giggled nervously. A

15

lot of people would have assumed so—assumed that a mother knew her daughter better than the first professor who came along. Steam rose from the coffee in their cups and gleamed like something ephemeral.

"Well, no," she said. "Actually, that's just the point. I don't know her."

"Well, who really can boast about knowing them?"

"Listen . . . I've only known Barbara for a few months."

He hesitated for a moment. "Well, then, we have an exception here," he said, in an attempt at humor.

He'd wanted to use a joking tone when this Myriam Thing-amajig's declaration popped out so disconcertingly, but quickly he realized that the woman wasn't saying anything other than what she was saying.

"Things like this do happen, you know," she said defensively. "Stop looking at me like that."

Although he was traveling light this time, he was out of breath by the time he reached the top of the hill. It was the price of peace of mind, the assurance that the place wouldn't attract crowds. He'd sit down a moment, he decided, smoke a cigarette, which would be incredibly delicious mixed with the fresh air against the background of ice-covered firs. He felt calm, relaxed. What a full day. He could boast about having warded off potential suspicions that could have singled him out. Right now, he had no cares. Not a soul had seen them together. Not a soul knew the nature of their relationship, not even her mother. It looked like Barbara really had held her tongue. He could breathe. Indulge in the pleasure of this wonderful blond tobacco.

His heart was beating. He kept several feet away from the

dark, mossy crevice—a rift of frozen, silent darkness. But, *whew*, what a relief. He congratulated himself for sticking to a strict discipline, always taking certain basic precautions when it came to the students. Now he could breathe. His defense system had worked. His security creed had paid off.

You had to be flat on your belly to get near the edge and look down into that black well of the unknown. When he thought again about how he'd nearly fallen into it before, he got goose pimples. One day he and his sister had found the body of a roe deer stuck halfway down, on a narrow projection that had probably snapped its spine. The next summer there was nothing left, not even bone.

The same thing was happening to Barbara's corpse. Although it was in shadow down below, you could still make it out perfectly—stopped as it was in its fall by a narrow overhang of damp rock in the shape of a door handle.

He lay there on his belly for a moment longer, his head suspended above the pit, wondering what to do next. Obviously, the chances of a hunter's, hiker's, or anyone else's eyes falling on the student's remains were scant. But not null. For a moment, crows flying circles in the blue sky captured his attention, and then he began reconsidering the problem posed by some stray tourist's or obnoxious mushroom collector's discovery of the body.

There was a way to reach it. A way to go down into that crevice if you were careful where you placed your feet—as far as he remembered—and reach Barbara's body. Just being cautious would do, checking his points of support, taking his time on the way down. The same for getting back up. But the effort would be worth it.

You had to do it right. His instinct had led him to get rid of the body, and getting rid of the body meant making it disappear—concealing it from all eyes, even if they were improbable. And yet, just as he was starting to realize, just as he'd feared, his work was only half done. He folded his glasses and put them away, thinking, *This is what happens when you do things too quickly.* It's true he'd been running very late that morning, had gotten rid of the girl fast, and left without turning around to look, to go give his course on John Gardner and moral literature. But that was no excuse. He hadn't shown much competence, that's all; in the end you often paid the price for your blunders.

The inside surface was steep and slippery. Luckily, he was wearing a good pair of shoes and more or less understood how to go about it; he'd served in the mountain infantry. A few stones crumbled under his feet and went flying into the pit. To lower the risk factor, he flattened himself as much as he could against the side and descended cautiously. The willies came with age, he thought to himself as he inched toward her body, the willies came with the consciousness of death.

When he got a foothold on the cornice, he realized he must look like he'd been rolling in mud. He was a real mess, he thought, grimacing, before twisting toward the student's body, which had turned purplish gray. She seemed to be balanced on a kind of spur.

If he stretched out one leg, he could just reach her with the end of his foot. He pushed. With the tip of his foot. It was a matter of toppling her back onto her path toward the shadows, but the job wasn't as simple as that. Something was jammed. Stuck. Cold sweat flowed down the small of his back as he struggled to push the body to the bottom of the pit and swore

by all the devils, whimpered, gasped for breath. All of it shattered the silence of the forest, usually so serene except for the
cry of a distant bird or the rustling of leaves—it was like a joke,
set against the medley of grunts and moans that spewed from
the bottom of the dark grotto, which had been transformed into
an echo chamber.

Then, about to be overwhelmed by his own helplessness,
he threw the last of his strength into the battle, was reduced to
clinging to a root with the tips of his fingers, and a loud tearing
sound accompanied the toppling of the girl's body into the void.

"Hello?" a voice above his head cried out. "Hello there?"

He froze; his heart stopped beating.

"Hello?" said the voice again. "Anybody there? Everything
all right?"

He pressed himself into the shadows against the side, bit his
lip. Had to think fast. Make the right choice.

"Hey! Can you hear me? You all right?"

Suddenly he understood what he was dealing with. To keep
hiding wouldn't do any good. This was the type of person who'd
force a blind man to be helped across the street and was always
mixed up with something that had nothing to do with him.
Most of the leftie professors were cut from the same mold.

"A.O.K. It's all good," he answered, emerging into the light.

"You sure?"

*R*ichard Olso was head of the literature department, and he was all that was missing: Richard Olso getting mixed up in this affair, even a little. The last thing in the world you'd want.

Had he seen something? Noticed anything?

"Marc? What are you up to down in that hole, old man? What the hell are you doing?"

The guy took his time studying you with those suspicious eyes of his.

"Same thing you are," he answered, hoisting himself out of the crevice. "I had the same reaction you did. Thought I heard shouting, somebody calling out, but seems I was wrong, there was nothing there. My foot got stuck on the way back up. Anyway, I think everything's fine."

"Then it must have been you."

"Me?"

"Had to have been you I heard. I stopped when I saw your car and heard the racket you were making."

"I really like taking walks here," he answered, turning toward the woods, where the treetops sparkled in the orangey light of the sun. "This was our place in the old days. We covered every inch of it, Marianne and I. Our parents were into living in the country; our mother was a vegetarian, among other things. I really like coming here around the first days of spring. Sometimes the light's fantastic."

Richard's way of nabbing the directorship of the literature department amounted to a veritable scandal. He was younger than Marc, had less seniority at the school, and had only taught one shabby course in comparative literature. But Richard, and not he, had gotten the appointment, as sickening as that was.

The only thing that made their being under the same roof bearable and reestablished the balance, steadied the beam, was the popularity Marc enjoyed among female students, none of whom could stand Richard. "Especially since he grew a beard," they'd snicker. "That little pointed jaw it gives him. Hee hee." It really was that stupid goatee; they couldn't have been more precise. He agreed wholeheartedly.

"When I was younger," Marc declared, as they walked down to their cars, "I was fascinated by spelunking. I guess it stayed with me."

Because of having been shut up in the basement, he thought to himself, as he avoided the sheets of ice scattered over the path. Or in the laundry, with the coal and potatoes—whereas other families had been heating their houses with electricity or gas for a long time. He shivered.

Marianne had lit a bunch of incense sticks on the ground floor. It was her privilege since it was her territory; but as time passed, their musky scent occasionally gave way to a strong odor of church. She mocked his half-hearted complaints about it and seemed to take a wicked pleasure in tainting the house, all the way up to the floor above, where he lived. There was a good deal of smoke floating in the air. Before he'd even hung up his muddy parka in the hallway, he'd started coughing.

She was in the living room. Afternoon was almost over; and light gilded the volutes. She was wearing one of his shirts, a striped one he'd looked for and couldn't find.

"Doesn't all this irritate your throat?" he asked.

Absorbed in examining some documents, which she was initialing with the speed of a submachine gun, she gave him a vague shrug.

"I ran into Richard," he announced. "Don't know what that idiot was up to in the woods, but I ran into him. You'd think he was following me, had me under surveillance or something."

"Yeah? Why would he do that?"

"Hmm? How would I know? Maybe he's thinking of giving me my walking papers? Trying to catch me in the act of something? Don't know if I'm going to put up with it much longer. They obviously want to downsize, get rid of people, that's no mystery. Why would this fucking campus ever want to buck the trend? Sorry. Excuse my vulgarity. But you know very well what I'm talking about. That little faggot Martinelli who's been president for the last year, the one who says amen to everything coming from Richard. I know, excuse my vulgarity. But it's true. Richard could easily have my head. He doesn't do it because you're here. That's the only reason. I don't have the slightest illusion about it."

He screwed up his face in reaction to the acrid smell in the air. "I know you've heard about it. Don't play innocent."

"What do you want me to do about it?" she answered, without raising her eyes. "I'm not responsible for that kind of thing."

23

He let out a small snicker. "Pardon me. Don't tire yourself out," he said.

She sighed. "Really, you're laughing at *me*?" She set down her pen. "We're talking about your little ploys, I assume. Do you think I'm deaf and blind?"

He studied her for a few seconds—long, heavy black hair; sparkling, determined eyes; pale lips; and he realized that he mustn't count on coming out on top. A few hours before he'd held the wrist—that shapely, white wrist—of Barbara's mother. The scene began replaying in his mind lewdly and made him lose track of the conversation—taking over suddenly, surprisingly, like a misstep hurrying toward the abyss.

Meanwhile, under the cloud of myrrh escaping from a handful of sticks stuck in sand and curling toward the ceiling, Marianne had gone back to her writing. "I know what I'm doing," she declared. "I have my reasons."

In the past, he'd go outside with her and show her there weren't any bad spirits hovering over the house; nowadays he didn't take the trouble. Marianne was a big girl.

He wasn't the only one who'd noticed this. Richard had started at the university two years before and had immediately gotten one unique idea into his head: becoming Marianne's lover, possessing her. From that time on, he'd never stopped stalking her. In that appalling way of his.

Which Marianne resisted, apparently, as far as he could tell. Until there was proof to the contrary. You didn't have to be a famous scholar to come to the conclusion that this guy was worthless; but sometimes women had baffling, inconsistent reactions—which it made sense not to trust.

He decided to change the conversation because the subject

had a way of making sparks fly. He told her about the interview in his office with the detective who was investigating the student who'd mysteriously disappeared.

"You know, I don't think the police are making any headway. That's my impression, anyway. That Barbara really seems to have, um . . . vanished into thin air."

She looked up at him. He kept his unruffled demeanor. If he'd seemed nervous during the forty-eight hours following the death of the girl, he was going about it differently now, had gotten his cool back, could control every muscle of his face, and was constructing a mask that could confront anything without the slightest effort, whenever the situation called for it. "We could have done without that kind of publicity," he went on, "don't you think? I'm talking about our image. I wonder if a hurricane hitting the campus wouldn't have been better."

She began collecting her things. She had a meeting with Martinelli coming up and would try to find out more about that downsizing rumor—if he didn't mind getting out from underfoot and letting her prepare for it. This didn't prevent him from following her to her bedroom, although he did stop at the threshold. "I think you should talk to our union representative," he went on, "and he'll tell you if it's something I'm imagining. Listen closely. It might even be edifying." She let her trousers slide to the floor and slipped into a skirt. "But don't count on their scruples," he added, his mind already elsewhere.

*S*he'd married Barbara's father six months earlier, around mid-September. They'd spent Christmas together before he left for Afghanistan, from which he rarely sent any news. "It wasn't that easy with Barbara," she mentioned. However, both of them were making an effort, and the forecast wasn't all doom and gloom; each day added to a budding relationship.

"Listen, Myriam, it's obvious what you want to talk about," he said assuredly. "It's easy to imagine what you're feeling. The incredible frustration." This time, the cafeteria was jam-packed and buzzing like a hive. "But, whatever the case, I have something to tell you," he went on. "I want to tell you she definitely would have made an excellent writer, I'm sure of it, and I mean that sincerely, and I owe it to myself to say it to you. We're going to miss out on something."

He wasn't in the habit of making such pronouncements about a student; the occasions were so rare he'd ended up forgetting that they'd ever existed—but the poor woman seemed so in need of comfort. And there was no doubt about it: Barbara had shown talent as a writer. A good enough writer. "I'm not saying this to please you," he added, touching her wrist again. "I absolutely must make that clear. You're going to see how competent her writing was. You'll see the potential she had. How well put together it was."

Myriam lived in the city, near the lake. He went by her place the next morning and slid about twenty sheets of paper into her mailbox—the last work Barbara had handed in, on a remarkable level for a woman that young. The trees were coming into bud above the sidewalks, and so were the hydrangeas; a few particles of pollen had begun spinning in the air. This girl would have reached greatness around 2020, he was willing to bet, because it wouldn't have taken her ten years to reach maturity, five or six, maybe. Becoming a good writer before thirty was pure fiction, with a few rare exceptions. Thirty's the absolute minimum, he'd explain right away to his students. Do you think a person learns to fool around with words in a day, or even a hundred, that the gift you'll need will suddenly fall from the sky? Listen to me, I'll be frank: figure on twenty years, twenty years before you start to hear your own voice, before you start going about it in some way. So, to put it briefly, if some of you nourish vague illusions in that respect, I'm happy to encourage them; but what I'm saying, my friends, is don't hope for anything serious, or expect anything powerful or staggering; in fact, don't expect anything that's really worth the trouble for the next twenty years—and don't forget it. We're talking two decades. Listen, those of you who have no affinity for sacrifice, just give up now. Good, I wrote my name at the top of the blackboard. Useless to look for it on Wikipedia. I'm not Michel Houellebecq. Sorry about that.

He found a note from Richard on his desk. About a spring assessment, totally informal and totally unrealistic; but Richard imposed such things on a regular basis. They were minor vengeances, small, detestable punishments he inflicted on the brother of the woman turning him down. Pitiful.

He smoked a cigarette while taking a few notes for the drudgery to come—when it was a question of contemporary literature, Richard Olso's taste was the pits. Unbelievable, but true. Really. And this was the man who'd been appointed head of the literature department.

How could they have chosen an imbecile like Richard instead of him? How could he keep from asking himself such a question? "Can I smoke?" he asked, as Richard shook his head and pointed to a chair. He defied the interdiction and lit one up. Richard could have had him thrown out of his office by the campus guards but didn't do it; and holding back like that was, apparently, harmful to the health of Richard's stomach— judging by the number of blister-packaged tablets of Inipomp 40mg littering his path.

This time, however, it became clear quickly enough that the reason for Richard's summons had more to it than the exercising of his famous power. "Okay, who's this woman?" he came out with. "The redhead in the cafeteria."

"Redhead? You see her as a redhead? Barbara's stepmother. Barbara, the student who disappeared."

"I know who Barbara is. I think I know everything that happens here, old man. What does she want? Tell me what she wants . . ."

"Her husband's in Afghanistan. We've sent soldiers over there. It's obvious that the Taliban have taken back the country."

"Fine, listen. Now listen to me. I'm asking you to keep your distance from her. We have to be careful. You have no idea the number of problems a mother, even a stepmother, can cause us.

All she has to do is throw a fit, start a scandal, and our rating could tumble, just like that. You know what it would mean for enrollment. Such a situation hardly lends itself to it, seems to me. We all have to fight to hold on to our professional positions."

"I know. But let's make sure we understand each other, Richard. What a reputation you're inventing for me. You've gone too far in my opinion."

"You're a charmer, Marc. You're nothing but one hell of a charmer, that's all there is to it. Don't tell me you're not."

They looked each other in the eye. He shrugged, crushed out his cigarette. You couldn't have everything in life. Certainly a department head had a more comfortable salary, and the power that came along with it, especially in these uncertain times, had to be very enjoyable. Yet attracting women, turning the heads of widows, students, housewives, and holding on to that gift, appealing to these fucking women before you even opened your mouth, without putting the slightest effort into it—*well*, he said to himself, *now there was something that gave pause for thought.*

He wouldn't have traded places with Richard. There was no sense thinking about it for hours. Ten or so years ago, his life had changed. It made a 180-degree turn the day he realized how something that seemed so complicated was really so easy. Things took on a different cast. And what a relief that had been! What a profound rebirth, in fact.

From there to thinking he wasn't against extending his hunting grounds to mothers, to the parents of students and the like, was a step he took easily. But his opinion wasn't important. He certainly wouldn't have traded places with Richard Olso, bitter and frustrated as Richard was.

"You attract them like flies to honey, don't you?" Richard snickered. "Don't tell me you don't. You seduce 'em by the dozens, right?"

It was sunny spring weather, bright and cold, and the scenery he could see through the big plate glass windows—those immense fir trees, the reflections on the lake, the snow that still lingered on the heights—were more conducive to contemplation than to any desire to be at loggerheads with the department head; those exquisite yachts darting by on silvered swells, those gulls, speedboats.

"Richard . . ." he said with a forced smile. "Richard, one of these days I'll stick you with a slander suit, you know. That'll settle it."

"What?" clucked the other, feigning bewilderment. "Am I inventing something? Huh? You have the nerve to say it's not true?"

It was time for another cigarette. There were occasions when he would have rolled on the ground for a Winston.

"Please," soothed Richard. "I'll let you go in a minute. Please."

He gave in, put the pack back in his pocket. He could still hold out for a few minutes. Finding work again wasn't ever easy, and he knew there were certain lines not to cross when it came to Richard, if he didn't want to become part of the shipwrecked legions. Revolting as the equation was.

"In any case, old man, don't go looking for trouble. Evil tongues are lying in wait. There'll come a moment when I can't back you up any longer. Marianne's aware of it. For example, get nabbed playing ladykiller with a student's mother—a missing student, no less—and I won't be able to do a thing for you, and I mean nothing. And you'll get pinched one day or another, that's for sure. I know it. We observe a certain discipline around here. I don't mind admitting it. But we're not about to change rules that have proven themselves up to now. Read my lips. We expect all professors to set an example, old man, and you know it."

"Am I being reprimanded for something? Does inviting a woman to drink coffee call for the disciplinary committee?"

"All right, Marc, you're not a bad guy, but I know you better than you think. I'm doing my best to warn you. I don't want Marianne to be able to reproach me for not warning you. You're your own enemy, old man, oh, yes you are."

Then Marianne parked and walked rapidly across the lot with a pile of files under each arm. He and Richard followed her with their eyes. She headed straight for the administrative buildings.

He took advantage of this to get away quickly from Richard, who was gently nodding his head in Marianne's direction. Teachers could form couples with teachers—no problem—the practice was widespread, even encouraged, around here; but that didn't mean teachers could form couples with students, or their parents. It was the law. Nobody wanted any hassles. Nobody thought about mixing categories. No sensible member of the community.

Midafternoon he gulped down some soup in the cafeteria and, just as he raised his eyes, there she suddenly was, sitting down across from him. He gaped at her for a moment, while she smiled faintly at him. "Of course you're not bothering me," he said, "not at all. Is there something I can get you? What'll you have? I recommend the pumpkin soup, it's delicious." He watched as she sashayed toward the pallid-looking food, carrying a metal tray. As a rule, you had your work cut out for you if you wanted a soup worthy of the name in this cafeteria—despite all the complaints he'd addressed to the administration, to no avail, of course. But there were a few sparks of genius, some flawless flashes, like the soup in question.

Myriam served herself a large bowl. It was cold outside; soup was perfectly appropriate. She'd waited a long time before marrying, a very long time; and when she'd decided to, as she neared fifty, when she'd finally decided to take the step, her husband had been sent to the other side of the world. Less than three months later. And that was that. He had to dodge bullets even while she was speaking to him. She wondered if she ought to consider it a punishment.

"You understand, don't you?" she said, staring at her soup.

"I'd do as much, believe me. I'd pester people, I really would, I promise you. Hold on now, I say it's completely natural." He bent and touched her wrist. She gazed up at him. "Have you read what she wrote?" he went on. "The mastery's amazing. The correct proportion of down-tempo and speed. Clarity and vagueness. It's so impressive, you know. I was about to give her a B+. A current passed between us, almost immediately. Sometimes I'd say to the others, 'Take her example and show a little proof of an ear when you write. Just about any idiot can tell a story. The only thing it's about is rhythm, color, tone. Take your classmate's example. Don't miss the mark. Above all, be good painters, good musicians.' Too bad such speeches always put them to sleep."

He watched her carry the first spoonful to her mouth. She hesitated.

"You're saying to yourself, 'Then doesn't this woman have

anything else to do with her days?' You're saying to yourself, 'What does she gain by doing this?' I really don't have an answer."

He was tempted to touch her wrist again to verify that it really was she producing that altogether astonishing sweet electric current traveling all the way to his shoulder as soon as he laid a finger on her.

"I think I feel a little alone," she finished, sighing. "You must find me unbearable."

"But what an idea, marrying a sergeant, of all things. A sergeant. The world is being torn apart, isn't it? Personally, I wouldn't take up a military career these days. Not on your life. Even if I were twenty. Especially if I were twenty. On the other hand, it's steady work, and I certainly understand that. I know that isn't a moot point. We all know it. All you have to do is take a look at the state of the auto industry. What's happening to our retirement packages."

"I've started to talk to myself when I'm alone. Or I leave the radio on. Do you know that I'm finding it harder and harder to remember what my husband looks like? Can you imagine? Can you believe it for a second? I think Barbara was preventing it. Keeping him from evaporating completely. Keeping the process from reaching its end. She was a link."

*Y*ou couldn't marry somebody in the military and then complain that the guy wasn't keeping regular hours. Marianne came out with this idea as the setting sun trembled over the lake. They were clearing the table. They'd dined early because Marianne wanted to go back to work. They did the dishes. She washed and he rinsed. Next they went to the living room to finish the bottle of chardonnay. She planted some more incense.

"Everybody saw you in the cafeteria."

"I know. We weren't trying to hide."

Before sitting down, she plumped up a few couch pillows. Quite firmly. Then she held out her hand. He brought her glass. As he'd talked about his encounter with Myriam he'd lit a fire, and now the flames crackled.

"What are you getting at?" he sighed as he sat down next to her. "I can't address one word to a woman anymore without your imagining God knows what. Don't you think you're going too far?"

By way of response, she held out her feet, declared that she'd been standing since dawn and that her ankles were swollen—underfloor heating disagreed with her. He massaged them.

When he sensed her relaxing, he raised the point that the fate of that woman was hardly enviable. "It doesn't surprise me she looks for someone to talk to. It doesn't surprise me for a second. Obviously she's lost, wants nothing, just to talk about Barbara, nothing else. It probably does her some good. Just talking about it. Nothing more. Should I have sent her packing? Turned my back? Tell me who would have had the heart to do that. Put yourself in my place for a minute."

She rarely batted an eyelash when he was busy with her ankles. She closed her eyes, and her face took on a much softer expression, which made her almost unrecognizable—as gloomy and tense as she was most of the time. For the time being, she was floating. Filled with satisfaction. So much so that, for the moment, she stopped looking for a quarrel and gave herself up to the massage—he had a real gift for it. Outside, the wind blew through the silvery darkness, and stars sparkled on the lake.

He went out to get a log. Shivered. Filled his lungs with freezing air. For a long time. In the distance below, to the west of the city, were the lights of the campus; then those of the airport, on the Swiss side; then the absolute blackness of fields of beets; and finally, the silhouette of the mountains against a background of night, their white, still-frozen noses. He lit a cigarette. Mixing pure air with nicotine, as night fell, was by far the best you could hope for in terms of subtle intensity. What a magnificent machine we sometimes inhabit, he'd then tell himself.

Fortunately, Marianne smoked, too. The odor of stale tobacco didn't bother either of them when they woke up in that house; every inch of it was impregnated with nicotine particles—especially in winter, because they didn't disagree about any need to open the windows to air things out, and especially these last two winters, for reasons of economy. Heating would soon become a luxury. His only minor concern came from the fact that she smoked dark tobacco. Every cloud she spewed had the form and density of a big, smooth pillow that took hours to dissipate into the air, but he refused to come off as a bad sport or quibbler or be petty about the issue. Both of them were stinking up the house. In equal proportions.

He loaded the log onto his shoulder, careful to avoid the back sprains that usually threatened men over fifty and that could turn the most robust of them into respectable-acting stuffed dummies. The day after he'd carried Barbara to her final resting place, there had been some warnings, several needle-like pains shooting through his lower back—as he first stepped out of bed and then during the car ride; a third time while writing at the blackboard; and finally, that evening, as he tried inspecting a washing machine that refused to function. He'd let out a short cry and yanked his head out of the porthole.

He came back in, shook his feet. Marianne had put on her glasses and plunged into her writing work, a cigarette in her mouth. He poked at the fire under the log. Turned and exposed his lower back to the heat of the flames. Microwaving a wet towel for three minutes was obviously a better remedy, but he didn't need it yet, the pain was lurking but hadn't hit—Voltaren, Darvocet, and Tetrazepam were his three religions in case of an attack. Chardonnay, too.

When he was done to a turn and taking a step toward the stairs leading up to his floor, she looked up at him. She often stopped him just as he was leaving. She hadn't always been like that, but aging isn't an improvement for anybody.

37

Philippe Djian

She took on a surprised look. "You're not going to kiss me?" she said.

He came up to her and bent down. She hadn't found a better way to verify he wasn't soaked in any particular odor, such as perfume, which would have immediately given him away; but he pretended not to notice her furtive sniffing.

Had she ever harbored anything but ordinary doubt when it came to him? Had she ever caught him red-handed? He'd learned to be discreet. He'd also been very careful not to get a swelled head about his serial successes and kept extremely vigilant. His last adventure was proof of it. Nothing could be traced back to him because he'd been so prudent until the end, and the result testified to this. Essentially, adopting good discipline was the simplest plan of all, following a few basic rules. No one wanted problems, to become the victim of a mishap. He'd done the only thing he could have done and refused to feel guilty about anything at all in such circumstances. He wasn't sorry about a single detail. Nothing contradicted his scrupulous analysis of the situation. His instincts had been right. There was no way to bring back a dead man. Or rather, a dead woman.

At times the wind in the fireplace howled like a dog covered with fleas, and the big windows trembled a little. He kissed her on the temple. She froze for three seconds, pen in air.

He took advantage of it by getting back to his bedroom. It was almost midnight. The light in the room revealed the nearest fir trees bending under gusts, the electric wires vibrating like whips, the rosebushes being manhandled, the spasms of the hedge, and the stiffness of the windsock in the form of a catfish from an Internet order mistakenly addressed to him. Thrilled by the object after unwrapping and examining it, he'd immediately made it his, denied having gotten it.

He lit a last cigarette, thinking of the one he'd light tomorrow morning, which he was lusting after already. A man certainly could have a few vices without needing to be ashamed of them, he reckoned. The ordeals you went through in a lifetime certainly gave you the privilege.

He stood there a few minutes without moving, watching the wind blowing and listening to the last third of "The Purple Bottle" coming from his earphones.

Then his telephone rang. It was she. Myriam. It was a little late to be discussing Barbara, it occurred to him; but he made an effort to see it from her point of view. He didn't have class the next day and therefore had no reason to get up early. He let it ring. Held his breath. Looked at his watch. At the end of one minute and twenty seconds, just before his lungs exploded, he answered.

There was something completely amazing, disconcerting about it. A few hours earlier, Richard had called him a charmer, and he had to face facts. His success with women was growing ever greater. What difference was there between the time when sleeping with a student was such an awkward, restrained, and easy-to-spot operation that it could take an entire school year, and today, when a woman called him in the middle of the night after only three informal encounters and was murmuring at the other end of the line?

Time and again, he'd looked in the mirror for what had changed in him, but what he saw wasn't too encouraging. He was missing some hair, the ones on his chin were turning gray; the lines in his face were deepening, and his eyes teared in the cold—to name but a few—to the extent that everything seemed to be going in the wrong direction; and yet, strangely, it wasn't doing that at all. On the contrary, everything seemed easier. He'd acquired genuine confidence in this realm. Sometimes he almost felt nonchalant about it.

"No, Myriam, you're not bothering me," he'd said, and climbed into bed in the dark with the telephone pressed to his ear and the small of his back propped up by a pillow, taking advantage of the time to clean his glasses. She had a pleasant, rather low voice. She asked him if he was doing anything special over there—now, at this precise moment—and he answered, yes. Which provoked a long silence on the line, broken by sounds of breathing, until she whispered, "Very well. In that case, good-night." And she hung up.

*H*e spotted her from time to time in different places, walking across campus, or even in the city, but she kept her
distance—she'd abandoned a nearly full shopping cart to avoid
being next to him at a mini-market checkout and had even
gotten off the bus another time. They exchanged only furtive
glances. When one of them smiled weakly, the other didn't, and
vice versa.

It started to make him think he'd been wrong and didn't
have the sex appeal he'd thought he had, which threw him into
a sense of deep turmoil mixed with sadness.

One morning Richard Olso came into his class and whispered a few words in his ear. He bounded out and rushed toward
the main building from which the flag of the European Union
and the university coat of arms fluttered. The trouble was coming from the library.

The firefighters were there. They were putting away their
equipment. Marianne was huddled in a chair, wrapped in a
blanket that looked like aluminum foil, and she was pale as a
corpse. Had she fainted? Of course. What else? When you eat
nothing but cottage cheese, zero-percent fat content, what else
could happen to you? How could you keep from conking out

at the top of a stepladder and just miss smashing your skull to smithereens?

He held her tightly against his shoulder. If she was incapable of eating anything else, there was nothing she could do about it. Blaming her didn't make sense. He thanked the firefighters. "Have her eat a good steak," declared the youngest, packing up the first-aid kit. He nodded. Marianne's hand in his was still cold and reminded him of gloomy events lost in the jungle of their childhood. "Anyway, all's well that ends well," declared Richard, gazing lovingly at her. "But Marianne, I might as well tell you, you gave us a terrible fright. Oh, c'mon now, be nice, and don't ever do that again, okay?"

She gave him a sheepish gesture of assurance with a still-weak white hand, while her brother slid a cigarette between her lips and resolutely conducted her to the parking lot. Spring had arrived two or three days ago, and the mimosa was in bloom; so were the hydrangeas.

"Let's not make a mountain out of a molehill," she declared as he pulled out. "And keep the car on the road, would you?"

He let out a nervous chuckle. "Just wondering what the two of you were doing together in the library."

"Pure chance. Don't be an idiot."

He shifted down and revved the motor before launching into a sharp turn where there was no guardrail. The shock absorbers creaked. The sun was already high, and as they drove, birds flew away from their path, cheeping as if fleeing an army on the march.

"I'm getting nauseous," she said.

"What? Sorry?"

"If you keep driving that fast, I'm going to be sick."

"What?"

He pulled to the shoulder immediately, popped out of the Fiat, made it around the car in three bounds, and opened her door. "Marianne, please. Don't upchuck in my car. Please. Make an effort this time. Lean out. Want me to help you lean out?"

She declined his offer. There was a very nasty-looking bump on her temple. She gave him a gesture meant to say she was okay. "Really?" he said with a glimmer of hope in his tone. "It's gone? How do you feel? You sure? Sure-sure?" In her survival blanket, she looked like a lush of about fifty he'd picked up at the edge of the road.

The surrounding woods were silent, and as the motor cooled down, it clattered like a skeleton. He decided to let her get some air. It certainly couldn't do her any harm, if a gust of wind didn't blow her away, given her obviously weak condition. He felt a little ashamed about not having been more observant, not noticing that she wasn't doing well—and God knows that the zero percent was an important clue to which he'd remained blind, having had other fish to fry.

He should have spotted all of it, her paleness, for example, the fact that she was happier sitting down than she usually was and that she was talking less, but his mind had been elsewhere—irrevocably.

"Are you all right? You'll be all right?" he asked.

"Obviously," she uttered, annoyed. "Give me a cigarette."

He lit two and handed one to her. The air was cold, but the sun was out. On the lake, a Lilliputian regatta was involved in some dispute. "I'm going to order in, all right?" Without waiting for an answer, he began dialing.

When they got home, he offered his arm for the walk from

the front seat of the Fiat to the living room couch, which he quickly swept clear of its magazines, TV guides, and literary thingamajigs so that she could stretch out.

She claimed she felt all right now and didn't need any help, and that it was too early for bed. He maintained that she'd done enough today, that her only job was to rest until evening, and that he didn't want to hear another word about it—she shouldn't even try.

"Eating a little raw fish will do you good," he declared, settling her among the pillows. "Some raw meat, too, by the way." They agreed on a cigarette, then were silent as the sun set behind the dark crests and inundated the horizon with a gilded mist.

"I'm going to the drugstore. I'll bring you some videos. What would you say to a good series?" They'd watched *Twin Peaks* together in similar circumstances, one summer that had left her weakened and absolutely ready for some long water-therapy sessions at La Baule or peaceful walks in Tuscany, entirely at their own expense. The emergency had required all of that, and he wondered what he'd do if Marianne's health called for new outlays of the same order. Their number of credit cards had fallen sharply—Diners Club had just canceled his, and HSBC was refusing to reconsider the line of credit they'd been given during the period when the world was rolling in it.

The thought was perplexing, and he brooded about it. Then the delivery person from Matsuri rang and he put it out of his mind—*eating Japanese is becoming a luxury,* he thought, shaking his head as he paid.

"I don't want to see anything left when I get back, not a crumb," he uttered as he put on his parka. "Don't try getting up before I do. Just relax. Don't go smashing your skull a second time."

She shrugged. "Come on, this is stupid, I'm fine . . . ," she sighed distractedly, checking out the contents of the bag from the corner of her eye. They'd brought those tasty little things made with tuna (the *Thunnus obesus* variety) and salmon (from nurseries in Norway), which were making her mouth water but turning her stomach at the same time. Whatever the case, she was very careful not to put a single foot off the couch. Seeing that she was beginning to behave, he lowered his eyes to his parka and zipped it up in one stroke. Time to leave, and it got cold out there at night early.

Jets of vapor streamed from his mouth as he walked through the door and back to the Fiat, which was starting to gleam in the moonlight. His phone rang. "Whatever you do, bring back cigarettes," she told him. "Whatever you do, don't forget that." He turned toward the house. The windows were lit up, but he couldn't see her. "Right now I'd rather you eat than smoke," he answered belatedly as he drove down toward the city, using low gear instead of braking.

Ten minutes later, he pulled into the shopping mall parking lot and went into the pharmacy, where he stocked up on bandages, Zopiclone, and Bion 3 with ginger. The stores were about to close. Security guards were starting to walk up and down aisles flanked by enormous, ferocious-looking dogs.

He was examining an antiaging cream by Biotherm—Age Fitness Power 2 with olive leaf—when he noticed Myriam opposite him, at the eyeglass shop across the way. *She certainly has a gift for surprise appearances*, he thought. He hadn't spotted her for several days, and at that moment, it occurred to him that he'd kind of missed her.

But the sound of a squabble attracted his attention—near

the phone store, they were ejecting a young, shaggy-haired guy who'd already slipped into his sleeping bag with the intention of spending the night right there. When he turned his attention back to Myriam with the beginnings of a smile, less than a few seconds later, as he prepared himself for news of the sergeant if that had to be, she was gone. Had disappeared. Had been dreamed?

He certainly was no expert on ghosts, but he had dealt with his mother's for a long time—nerve-wracking—so after all these years he stopped letting himself be thrown by such phenomena, duplicitous as they were.

He calmly finished his errands. The supermarket was emptying out, and walking around deserted shelves wasn't at all unpleasant: reading labels, comparing prices, etc. He lingered a bit, not in the slightest upset by his hallucination.

The important thing was not to forget those cigarettes. The important thing was to bring back something to clean the wound—caused by the contact of the library floor tiles with his sister's temple, which had split open a bit and swelled up like a pigeon's egg. He had to focus, keep from being invaded. He had to act like he was driving a racing car, like the slightest second of inattention could put him into a tailspin—had to think of life as a race, keep his eyes fixed on the road. That was the plan of action he'd chosen, and carrying it out left hardly any room for ravings.

A kind of conversation pulled him out of his musing—a man pushing a mop more than six feet wide and towing a pail of liquid bleach on wheels told him the store was closing soon and that people had to go home now without trying to make a fuss.

Make a fuss? He was surprised for a moment, then followed the employee's eyes, which were looking at the cigarette he'd unconsciously lit.

Every time he tried to stop, he would start again with a vengeance, dragging Marianne down with him, and right now other safeguards were collapsing. The verdict was clear. Soon he'd be found smoking in a church or hospital or in the corridors of a sanatorium. Nostalgically, he thought of the days when you could do it in trains and planes and elevators, without so much as a thought of the worst, of the damage you were doing. He apologized. They knew him in this store because he left a good part of his salary here and didn't steal anything, break anything, so he was going to make it back to the exit without being taken straight to the police station or, more simply, having the shit kicked out of him first and then locked in a cell overnight to learn some respect for law and order.

He was one of the last customers; there was only one register open, and the poor girl left at it was yawning her head off. All around, salesgirls were closing their shops and hurrying to different locations in the night, like troopers on a mission. He wasn't sure he wanted to take the elevator, but finally stepped into it because, at this point, he'd nearly mastered his phobia about them breaking down, even if this particular car didn't inspire confidence and had the size and appearance of a beat-up cattle truck. The slightest self-mastery, he thought to himself, came only at the price of bitter struggle. Who could claim the contrary? How many people had inherited an easy world, could get everything they wanted?

The parking lot was on the last, open-air level. Halfway there, the elevator stopped with a jolt, broke down. The lights went out to the sound of a death rattle. He felt like a bullet had just hit him in the center of his chest or that he'd been struck by lightning. His legs gave way for a moment, he couldn't breathe, and his mouth got as dry as if he'd chewed plaster; but from deep inside he drew the strength to overcome the ordeal and grabbed his cell phone. Using it as a flashlight, he looked for the buttons on the elevator panel, especially the one for the alarm. He rang for emergency help, but nothing happened. Then he shouted out for it, also unsuccessfully.

Bent forward, his hands on his knees, he took some deep breaths. Then he straightened and turned back to the button panel, seriously manhandled it. His fist was still raised and his mouth full of curses when the light came back on and the elevator suddenly started moving.

He wiped his glasses and mopped his forehead while the tin can that called itself an elevator, into which he'd had the rotten luck of setting foot, hoisted him to his parking level. Despite the no-smoking sign, he lit up a Winston.

The elevator doors opened, and he saw the parking lot bathed in moonlight. The cold air swallowed him. There wasn't a soul to be seen at that hour; the place was deserted. Under a pristine, starry sky, he began walking to the Fiat. The air was biting. He winced.

Then he was victimized by that hallucination again. For the second time that evening he saw Myriam, and this time she was walking straight toward him.

"Listen I lost my car keys," she announced, avoiding his eyes. "Truth is, I've really lost my keys."

"Keys? Oh. You look frozen stiff."

"Am. Waited for you. I recognized your car."

"Well, believe it or not, I was trapped in the elevator."

"Listen, I thought you could drop me off. I thought, 'I'm going to wait for him and ask, find out.'"

"I certainly can. Get in. It would be a real pleasure. It's going to get cold again, all this week. That's what I heard. That pressure system can't seem to stabilize. Think it's a bad sign? We certainly will find out what the future has in store for us ...," he blurted out, opening the door for her.

As he was buying a ticket to exit the parking garage, he observed her from a distance. The machine kept refusing his card, so he felt irritated, and happy about her being there at the same time. This was nothing like his reaction to the various students he'd been involved with all these years. Not at all the same—no comparison. Despite the cold, she'd opened her window—rare were those who appreciated the bitter, pungent odor of old tobacco in the reduced space of a closed car. Now he had a full view of her profile, and he saw how extraordinarily strong it was.

His oldest conquest had been twenty-six the day they separated. Myriam was twenty years older. He knew as much as a baby would about such a new domain, but he also instinctually knew that nothing would get simpler or gain more clarity—not when it came to the heart of a woman—no matter how the two of them went about it.

He who expected nothing would never be disappointed. He not guilty of optimism would never suffer a fall. He who confronted the mountain patiently and humbly would arrive at his goals. He who didn't overestimate his powers was a formidable adversary. He found the exit ticket he'd bought earlier. Just one second of imagining how frustrated a sergeant's spouse could be when he was on maneuvers at the other end of the world might give him a stroke, it occurred to him as he climbed in next to his passenger, whose face had a faraway smile.

He who travels light won't arrive done in. He who doesn't live on hope won't die of exhaustion.

Night enclosed the world around them like a bell jar. The parking lot felt as if it were perched on the summit of a steep peak, like an eagle's nest. "We should put on some music," she said after a moment.

He folded his glasses and slipped them into his pocket. "Karen Dalton?" he suggested.

He leaned sideways so he could reach the glove compartment, glancing as he did at her thighs emphasized by silky pantyhose, the color of cream. It wasn't hard to imagine her in a bathing suit—or better yet, in her underwear. Not much more than forty-five years old. In peak condition. Intellectually mature. What more was there to say about it? Could you imagine a more perfect creation, more unnerving company?

The idea of awakening the interest of a person like her wasn't a turn-off; it was actually good for his self-esteem, he supposed—being able to interest someone with a mind, who had taste and experience in life. Suddenly he was struck by the mediocrity of his relationships with the student population. Sexuality hadn't made that world any less impermeable. Most of those women had turned out to be kind, clever, energetic lovers; but no real exchange had taken place, no real connection been made. Now he understood why.

Something inside him had opened up, hatched inside his chest—passing from childhood into adulthood provoked similar feelings. Something had slowly matured, a secret gestation that had produced a new man, born on that night. *After this*, he asked himself as he pressed the buttons of the CD player in search of that heartrending voice, *can I ever go back to the young girls I liked before? Will I lose all interest in them?* For one thing, as a professor, a person who spent the better part of his time with them, he wasn't especially looking forward to such a change—although it wasn't up to him. These things couldn't be controlled.

She placed her hand on his arm. "Isn't this a strange situation?" she said. "But I would do something like that. I'm exhausted, don't sleep well, so I'm not thinking very clearly."

"You know, when you touch me, I feel something like an electric current. Don't you?"

"No. I mean I don't know."

"Any news from your husband?"

She shook her head. He reached for the key to the ignition, but she stopped him again.

"I can't even remember his name anymore," she said, staring into space. "This morning I drew a blank. It took me several seconds before I could say it. . . . It's awful of me, I know, truly awful on my part. Disgraceful."

"No it isn't. Not on your life. Listen to me, Myriam, not on your life. No one forced him to have an army career. He's got only himself to blame."

"That electric current you mentioned, what is it?"

"That electric current I mentioned?"

"Yes."

"That electric current I mentioned?"

"Yes."

He felt his mouth becoming dry. It was cold outside, and so

was the inside of the Fiat, because he hadn't started the motor yet. His nose felt frozen.

"I'm afraid of us getting stuck in here," he said. "We'd better not linger. It happened to me once. Luckily, it was summer."

"Marc, if you only knew how much I'm longing for summer to start."

"It's coming. The buds are here. When you look up it's green."

The conversation was becoming surreal. They could have floated to the middle of the cosmos, to the dead center of night, lost themselves in the middle of nothingness. What difference did it make?

Now his heart was beating as if he'd begun jogging peacefully along the lake. No student had ever had such an effect on him. Karen Dalton was singing "Everytime I Think of Freedom."

"I love that woman's voice," he declared.

She nodded. Then she took his hand and pressed it to her cheek.

On such occasions, he said to himself, *you miss being the owner of an Audi A8 with leather interior.*

Now it felt like he was going as fast as the wind, at about 140 rpm. Despite the fact that he wasn't moving. An amazing phenomenon in itself.

Her lips brushed his hand, and she raised her eyes to his. "Do I kiss you?" she murmured. He nodded gently. She wasn't his mother, his sister. She didn't have to stop. His only regret had to do with how uncomfortable the Fiat was—unworthy of such a woman—but we don't always get what we want, and many of his relationships had been nipped in the bud because of a bad start, an inappropriate place, etc. There wasn't much you could do about it. It was just one gigantic crapshoot.

He thought briefly about the sergeant wandering among the stones of a rock-strewn desert, praying not to fall into an ambush, praying to keep alive.

He got home late. About two in the morning. That night, at the wheel of his throbbing motor, as he was driving through the silent forest, he felt as if he were sawing the world in two with an enormous chainsaw, awakening in his path the smallest field mouse, the tiniest creature, crow, worm. He'd lost a good part of his muffler, he was sure of it. And experience told him that, even if he finished the trip at the same speed and cut the motor, there was a fifty-percent chance she'd hear him arrive. Or she'd be waiting for him because she was in a state. Or else asleep, but listening with one ear.

"Do you know what time it is?" she said as he was getting ready to go straight up to his room.

She'd just used the remote control to turn the lights on in the hallway and had caught him with a foot in the air and a hand on the banister.

Then she turned on the lights in the living room, lowered the lamps, with the same device. "Well finally. Where'd you go?"

He waved the cigarettes and the stuff from the pharmacy in front of her. "Everything's here. Everything you wanted."

She dove onto the pack of cigarettes and nervously un-wrapped it. "Hello? Have you seen what time it is? There isn't a single lousy butt in this goddamn house. But I guess you think that's funny. After all, it only took you seven or eight hours."

"Calm down and listen. It so happens I was stuck in the shopping mall parking garage. That's what happened. The barrier came up out of the ground and blocked me from getting back down. Stuck. I was stuck up there all this time. That's the real story of what happened."

"Fascinating," she said in a grating voice. "What you're telling me is fascinating."

"I didn't have my phone. Or I would have called. I knew you were waiting. I smoke, too, you know. You don't have to draw me a picture. You think I'd have been capable of deserting you? You think I didn't know you were walking in circles like a rabid animal? Of course I noticed how long it was taking. And I was worried sick about it, but all of them were so slow I could have hung around all night in their damned parking garage."

"You smell sweaty. I can smell your body odor from here."

"Yeah, well, I'm not surprised. It wasn't a walk in the park. I mean, I was purple with rage. I came close to pounding that machine into the ground when it kept insisting my ticket to get out wasn't valid, repeating it ad nauseum. All that technology can end up driving you out of your mind, don't you think?"

He was surprised at the ease with which he handled the conversation, the way all the words came flowing from his mouth. The woman he'd held in his arms only a few moments before was still in them. His mind was so full of her that this conversation seemed like a miracle.

The next day, the same thing happened. Myriam was the first image to cross his mind, as soon as he opened his eyes from a deep, subterranean sleep.

He went downstairs and squeezed some oranges, made toast and buttered it, put some jam on it, and poured a bowl of rolled oats with maple syrup, because he was determined to keep an eye on Marianne's health, bring back a little color with the arrival of spring. He put all of it on a tray. Humming softly, he carried it into her bedroom. She was still asleep. Or faking it.

He put down the tray and decided to sit next to her in the dark. The smell of that room was truly disturbing—always had been. There was a morning odor in that room before Marianne rose, as if a part of her body had evaporated during the night and was floating in the tepid air.

He had a whole list of suggestions for her but did nothing more than open his mouth and keep it that way for an instant, before his lips rejoined. After lighting a cigarette, he took a notebook from his pocket and scribbled a few words to her. It was the beginning of a lovely, cool, luminous, day—a few crystalline rays pierced the gaps in the curtain. But the most amazing thing of all happened as he was writing those two or three sentences; in fact, just as he was tracing out each letter: once again, he saw a few fragments of his embrace with Myriam the night before in that miserable little car where they'd gone at it, and he was secretly shaken by these visions.

Not that he regretted giving in totally to the adventure, which he immediately classified among the best—sexually speaking. But he was aware of the measure of danger in it too, or rather, wasn't measuring anything at all. The truth was that he found himself at the edge of an abyss and was having a hard time forming an opinion about what had happened. About this unknown territory into which he'd wandered and about which he knew nothing. His only expertise came from the world of students, malleable types; beyond that he understood nothing. Had to play it safe. Myriam could change things dramatically,

55

irrevocably. His instinct could fathom it fully. His body clearly understood the message of the current, those subtle vibrations she was transmitting. His mind, on the other hand, seemed to be refusing to put itself on alert.

Just before he walked into class, Richard Olso stopped him in the hall for news about Marianne. "I want to be sure that you're doing what needs to be done, old man, I'd like to be sure of it." He added that he'd pay her a visit—today, even. If Marc saw nothing inconvenient about it. Both of them snickered self-consciously.

The department had organized a program of panels and meetings with professional Hollywood screenwriters, and everybody wanted to learn how to concoct a series or whatever else would rake in millions and bring with it the privilege of dining at Steven Spielberg's table—before having coffee with Nicole Kidman. He took advantage of his students' defection to go and get his muffler changed, in anticipation of more discreet destinations, should the need arise. Obviously, the wisest thing was not to see her again and forget her as quickly as possible—that is, if he had an iota of sense left.

Annie Eggbaum wasn't particularly attractive, but she could help him get back his equilibrium if he decided to. Her face was nothing special—bland, and quality or originality weren't present in her work. But she had a good body and was making use of lower and lower necklines as the year advanced.

Once he had his new muffler, he went back to his office. He was looking over the papers that some of the students had handed in when she leaned in toward him—chest first—and begged him again to give her those private lessons she so direly needed. No exaggeration there—the poor girl would never be able to write a single good sentence.

"Annie, listen. I don't know what to tell you. Stop bugging me. I truly believe these classes are a waste of time. You have no ear, and I'm afraid I can't do anything about it. Why are you insisting?"

"I'll work. I'll work twice as hard. Writing's a question of work. It's ninety-nine percent work. You say that all the time."

"I'm supposed to look after the one percent that's left, Annie, and that's something we can't avoid. It wouldn't be fun for either of us."

He gave her a cigarette. Part of his notoriety among students had to do with the fact that he was incapable of preventing anyone from smoking—when he wasn't busy encouraging himself to do the same.

"The hardest thing is admitting you're hopeless," he said with a shrug, stepping away from the desk. "It's really very hard . . . but everything depends on what you do with that idea, right? Some people would rather not set their standards too high in exchange for more of a guarantee. Don't you want that? Take a look at me. Do I seem unhappy? Listen to me, Annie, let it go. It's nothing to be ashamed of. Don't make yourself unhappy. Don't wait until you're my age to open your eyes. You're young, not damaged yet. Face facts. Face facts, young lady."

He wondered if she was about to sit on his desk, thought things were leading to that. The atmosphere was right, the hallways quiet, and to the east, the morning sunlight sparkled through trees bordering the campus. It was still cold, but most of the female students had already dusted off their miniskirts, and Annie hadn't chosen the longest. Quite a few teachers were complaining about the phenomenon, and their wives got together regularly at teatime to denounce such outrageous, unacceptable outfits, too prevalent at the arrival of spring.

Marianne herself wasn't the latest to take offense at the size of those scraps of cloth some dared wear, which weren't much larger than handkerchieves. Every year she had dwelled on the issue a little more viciously. Nor was he spared. Hypocritical, spineless, and willing as he was supposed to be, he was labeled a potential victim, a shell of a man who could be blown away by the slightest puff of air. The hint of bitterness in her words, her tone of reproach, clued him in to the fact that she was aging—that both of them were—but it still didn't mean she'd ever really caught him in the act.

"Class is in less than ten minutes," he said.

"That sounds about right," Annie answered. "Listen, there's nothing I can do about it if my father's rich. It's not something I chose."

"Wish mine had been, come to think of it."

"Actually, it's not ten minutes. It's twenty. At the soonest. They're mesmerized by those types."

"Of course they're mesmerized. I figure they have to take notes. Which of us hasn't eyed the other side of the Atlantic at least once? You're not fascinated with Martin Scorsese? You wouldn't like to be able to use his brain to write a screenplay?"

"Is he here?"

"Of course he isn't. Martin Scorsese? Wake up, Annie. Martin Scorsese here? With what money? Look at what they give to Culture. Peanuts, Annie. Sometimes I'm ashamed of this country."

Her bosom was freckled.

"Listen, Annie, we'll talk about all this another time if you really want to because, whether they're mesmerized or not, I can hear your classmates coming. I think you'd better get off my desk. I think you'd better. Be nice. I'm going to see what I can do to help you. What would it be? Once? Twice a week?"

He devoted part of the afternoon to cooling them down, worked up as they were by one of those Hollywood types, who must have been the writer of a successful series, or big-budget films, or best sellers—somebody on the way up with a house and pool, who got splendiferous fees, prizes, awards. The Golden Age was over, but they didn't want to hear it. He passed for the perfect wet blanket and spoilsport, the soon-to-be retired. He smoked a cigarette for a little peace and quiet while he made them work on a short dialogue from *Doctor Strangelove*.

But if he was thinking he'd get Myriam out of his mind that way, he was wrong.

After class, he made a detour through the cafeteria. The day was ending, gilding the edges of the windows. The room was nearly empty. He had a brief exchange with the waitress, who was busy filling up the little jars of mustard on the tables, but she hadn't seen her, hadn't seen Myriam that day. He got up and silently served himself another coffee.

Annie Eggbaum reappeared just as he was deciding to leave.

"First of all, I hated that movie," she declared.

It was a very, very black mark against her. But at least she had nerve. Then she ended up admitting that she didn't detest it that much. He felt under the table for her knee, which wasn't to say that Myriam had been erased from his mind.

He glanced around. The only person left was the waitress, now busy with the saltshakers. Dusk was setting in. He wasn't sure what Annie Eggbaum had swallowed, but she seemed to want to devour him with her eyes. She was rubbing her knee against him without the slightest restraint, with an insistence that almost seemed bad-tempered.

It had to be because of a bet. Or too many vitamins. How could you know what a girl was capable of inventing?

"Are you driving?" he asked, in a lowered voice. She shook her head. He looked into her eyes. "Wait for me in front of the parking lot," he said, after a moment of hesitation. "I'll be there in five."

He'd acted in haste before, but not to the point of being spotted with the wrong kind of company; and recently, caution had proved itself indispensable in the case of Barbara, which could have led to nothing but absolutely pointless hassles and harrassments when you took into account the police and their methods and the fact that they had put a stranglehold on Human Rights Watch and company.

The entrance door closed on Annie's heels after she stole a last glance in his direction. A wave of heat coursed through him. He blotted his forehead with a recycled paper towel and offered a cigarette to the waitress. She slipped it behind her ear. "For later," she said. They chatted a little, then he said good-bye.

There was a moon now. He walked outside and, keeping his head down, headed straight for the Fiat, his damp forehead immediately beginning to ice. The perfect way to catch a chill.

He got behind the wheel. Annie was standing on the sidewalk about a hundred yards away, in front of the service entrance to the cafeteria. It was lit by a streetlight with a yellow

glow, and the vision—a young woman waiting patiently—
quickened his breath. He switched on the ignition. True, Annie
had pressured him, and he wasn't going to pretend that hadn't
happened; Annie had thrown herself at him, but he didn't see
much risk in it. If it had to come to this to escape an infinitely
more awful, infinitely more dangerous threat, he was ready to
submit. His instinct for survival had developed considerably
these last years.

He pulled up along the sidewalk, and, once again, as he ap-
proached, enjoyed the appealing-looking body of the student
with the rich father—and with the future lover who was the
owner of the smallest car in the world. Just as he leaned over to
open the door for her, he saw the waitress behind her, coming
out in a hurry to smoke her cigarette.

He clenched his teeth. In a fraction of a second, his hand
changed its course and flattened itself against the button that
locked the door. His eyes crossed the waitress's as she flicked
her lighter, while Annie, very much in the foreground, frowned.

Straightening up, he bore down on the accelerator, taking
off immediately at top speed. Without a single glance in his
rearview mirror—Annie couldn't have been smiling, he told
himself—he slammed through the gears.

He felt bad for her. It wasn't going to be easy to come up
with a believable explanation for the dirty trick he'd played on
her. Obviously, he'd have to make the gesture of private lessons
to redeem himself.

It didn't matter what the job was, it had to be meticulous.
Things had to be done well. He had no intention of committing
such a ludicrous mistake. Because of that insane, intolerable
rule that stopped professors from going to bed with students,

you had to stay in the shadows at any cost; and this was something he stuck to, not letting anything get in the way. It didn't
matter what the job was, it had to be meticulous. Nothing could
ever come out of the shadows. Every man had to keep tabs on
his own security.

As he tore along the road to the cottage, the radio announced
new clashes in Afghanistan—more soldiers falling during new
ambushes along distant frontiers—and he thought immediately
of Myriam.

He'd never had relations with a woman of more than twenty-
six. As stupid as it was. It was certainly no great feat. Quite simply, the occasion hadn't presented itself. He hadn't looked for it,
either. His sister was enough of a cruel complication of existence.
He'd had enough of her complicating everything.

Not that Myriam had failed his expectations—on the contrary. Only women had better orgasms when they had feelings
for their partner. Obviously, it wasn't yet at that emotional
level; he mustn't exaggerate. But the rapport they'd had on the
backseat of his cramped car, acrobatic and crude as it may have
been, had literally enthralled him. He was still thinking about
it, feeling the greatest confusion—he'd had an incredibly long,
incredibly expressive ejaculation, which wasn't even the slightest
bit usual.

The Fiat climbed upward among firs and chestnut trees in
the feeble gleam of the yellow headlights of that year's make
of car. By now, the last traces of snow had melted; a light mist
had begun to hover above the clearcut areas—above meadows,
houses, sheep and cow pens, brushwood, fields, fallow land that
bordered the road embankments slanting toward the lake in the
gloom.

Living outside the city was a blessing—a way of keeping your head above water, of allowing yourself to breathe. He and Marianne had been born in that house. Their father was a teacher at that university. He'd bought the house at the beginning of the fifties, at a time when the price of real estate hadn't yet reached surreal sums and it was still available to ordinary mortals. Supposedly, their mother had lived her most beautiful years there— until the moment she became pregnant, first with Marianne and then, immediately after, with him. Holding Marc on one knee and Marianne on the other, their father had explained to them that their mother hadn't always been the woman they now knew. Then he'd begun to cry his heart out for not having intervened, for yet again having been so weak, for being a perfect creep.

Richard Olso's car was parked in the driveway. It was a red Alfa Romeo, tailor-made for his persona. As soon as the first sunny days arrived, he'd put the top down and stick one of his pathetic caps on his head. As he went by, the girls would burst into concealed laughter—nobody wanted to antagonize the head of the literature department as he grinningly drove at a crawl across campus, his arm resting on the windowsill.

In front of the entrance to the house, the vehicle gleamed idiotically under the porch light. Anyone who'd been brought up a little better would have parked a bit farther away, but Richard Olso wasn't a man to trouble with such subtleties. Unfortunately. For a moment, he imagined Olso becoming a sort of brother-in-law, in case Marianne gave in, and he shuddered yet again. Switched off the motor. Sighed.

The die wasn't cast yet, however.

Was there even a chance he could put up with a guy like that under their roof?

From outside, he glimpsed them near the fire in the living room, munching on chocolates. Almost instantly, his migraine came back. Migraines go hand in hand with annoyance. He went inside. Hung his parka in the hallway—next to a camel's-hair overcoat that didn't belong to anyone living in this house.

"You've got to watch your sugar. Richard, she has to watch her sugar, you know that."

"Just let her get a little of her strength back, old man, and don't worry about it. I think we have the situation under control."

"I can eat as many chocolates as I want," she declared, holding a ganache between thumb and forefinger.

It was obvious she was trying to punish him by acting unpleasant toward him and conspicuously friendly toward Richard, whose face shone with deep satisfaction.

Before ruling over the fates of members of the literature department, Richard had worked as a cultural attaché in the depths of Europe, where he'd caught a case of Lyme disease. This was the cause of his slight—but crippling—facial paralysis, the bitter fruit of one of those poorly treated diseases caused by ticks, which also gave him certain joint problems and, to top it off, stiffened his walk. It wasn't hard to imagine that a physique like that didn't exactly make it a cinch to turn heads. When you looked at it objectively.

And yet, Marianne. What could she possibly see in him? Why the devil was she letting him woo her so disgustingly, what kind of perversion was it covering up? What mental abnormality?

Marc decided to keep them company. After all, this was his home, and it was time to make Richard understand that the moment to leave had come because the house was closing up for the night and its inhabitants were going to bed. He sat down in a chair and yawned, refusing Richard's offer of chocolate.

"No thanks, it'll keep me from sleeping," he declared.

The moon outside shone in the cold air like a porcelain disc.

"Anyway, thanks for coming by, Richard. I parked so you could get out without any trouble, but if you're at all worried about it, here I am, at your service. Thanks again for stopping over. Personally, I'm exhausted. I have a migraine. And Marianne, I wouldn't say you've gotten much of your color back. You should get some rest. It's well past the time, you know. You were having trouble standing not that long ago. Don't overestimate your strength. We just scraped you up off the ground, remember."

Again, how could a woman like her be attracted—little as she claimed she was—to a man like that? A woman who usually showed such judgment, taste, diligence, intelligence. Did it have anything to do with the fact that Richard was the head of the literature department and Marc was under his control? Was that a turn-on? Could you exhibit such a mad passion for Nabokov and yet subsist on such paltry little scenarios?

She was his older sister, but didn't he deserve respect? Didn't he deserve to be spared humiliations and other betrayals of their routine after the thrashings he'd taken in her place out of a spirit of generosity? How many handfuls of hair had he lost, how many knockouts had he submitted to? Three, if you counted the time when he hadn't passed out but lay staring at the beaten-earth floor at the bottom of the stairs where that woman had thrown him, leaving him incapable of the slightest movement for minutes that felt endless, barely able to breathe and peeing in his short pants without being able to do anything about it in the state of shock he was in.

He deserved her complete respect. She shouldn't be pushing the joke too far. He stared hard at her. She resigned herself to lowering her eyes and reaching for her cigarettes. "Marc's right," she said. "It's late. Your chocolates did do me some good, Richard. Thanks for visiting. Thanks for caring about what happens to me."

"Listen. It's nothing special, Marianne. You know that. Whatever you want, just ask."

"You're too kind, Richard. But don't worry, I'll be back in stride very soon. Spring is going to help me. I'm going to start going to the gym. I'm going to sign up at one."

"If you want, I'll give you the address of the one I go to. I think it's the best one. Do you want me to take care of it?"

Their conversation went on like that for quite some time. It was incredible. Marc was laughing sarcastically about it for a long time after Richard cleared out at the wheel of his Alfa Romeo, swallowed up by the pale night. Incredible. Grotesque.

"I should have caught this on camera," he jeered. "I could have watched it again."

"You couldn't be more wrong. You've got an overactive imagination."

He caught the packet of cigarettes she threw at him in midair.

*T*he next day he got up early and went for a long walk through the woods and far into the surrounding soft green hills as a way of avoiding the temptation to go back into town in hope of running into Myriam, or maybe walk up her street, peek through her windows, or something to that effect.

Having his mind invaded by a woman like this was something new for him. He wasn't being invaded by fear, resentment, a desire for vengeance, or other lovely thoughts like the ones his mother used to inspire in him, or even the somber ambivalence his sister could evoke in him; he was being invaded by a pleasant, mysterious power that sometimes began churning like an incredibly beneficent, dangerous flood. It was incredibly new.

More than ever, walking seemed necessary. If you put the number of miles he'd traveled through these woods end to end, amidst these hills, over these streams, faults, and chasms, you'd lose your bearings. If he closed his eyes, he could still feel the leaves slapping against his face, rain and night falling on his terrible path one evening in November when she was chasing him with a pitchfork. But he could also see incredible mornings sunnier than gold coins, sparkling with light that forced you to squint, when he'd go swimming with his father in a stream so icy that his father ended up having to squeeze him in his arms until his teeth stopped chattering. Today the air smelled good— a mixture of cold earth and new grass.

For the first time since he woke up, he thought for an instant of Annie Eggbaum and the problems waiting for him when he reappeared on campus. He hurtled down a slope covered with dead, shriveled, dry gray leaves and got back on a path that passed above the road. Having no convincing explanation to give the student, or any he could be very proud of, he wagered she wasn't going to spare him her resentment. Anyone in her place would act like that. Anyone would cry out for revenge.

He held on to the idea of the private lessons she'd been clamoring for since the start of the year. He could come off as open to that; how much leeway he showed was pretty important. He could begin by giving her the gift of the first week and see what she thought of it. Raise a low grade for her from time to time to bring back her smile.

When he got near the pit, he glanced around and noticed nothing in particular, saw nothing, detected no smell coming from the damp, mossy darkness that plunged deep into the earth. Barbara's sleep was silent and peaceful, and you could only be overjoyed about it, for both of them. This pit certainly was the last word when it came to graves, the best you could want under certain circumstances. Its depth made it final, absolute. He threw in a few crocuses he'd picked up on the way and lit a cigarette, each one of which tasted more superb than the one before.

In the end, maybe he'd have to go to bed with Annie Eggbaum, he thought vaguely. It would be the only option if she took too hard-line a position and was counting on making him pay a high price for his rudeness.

The idea of managing a double affair made him nervous, produced a certain anxiety he couldn't dispel by smoking a cigarette outdoors—a Winston—on a pleasant spring morning. Obviously, some people were thrilled about confronting the unknown, hoping and praying for it, using it to trigger match-less orgasms; but not in his case, far from it. He'd had his fill of adventures, trembling, reversals, action, surprises, suffering, joy, etc., and wasn't rubbing his hands together or chomping at the bit while watching the approach of this ordeal. The unknown had no attraction for him—quite the opposite. The unknown seemed like a phosphorescent fog to him, as thick as pudding and bringing with it every possible snare, every imaginable problem. He knew.

For years he'd been hoping for stability. A lot of things had fallen into place as soon as he'd understood he'd never be a writer, a real one. It was better to know it. A tremendous rebirth for him. He knew the burden he'd been spared. Obvi-ously, something inside him was shattered, crushed; but what a relief when it came down to it, what freedom. Sometimes he shuddered at the mere thought of the staggeringly monastic life he'd escaped. Who'd return to handle a radioactive substance with bare hands until they were burned, or keep breathing in asbestos, being poisoned gradually, until the end result? No real writer escaped it. There was no exception to the rule. You couldn't ever envy guys like that. No one could understand your choosing to let your heart be devoured without even flinching. Most of his students thought it was a profession just like any other. Trying to make them change their minds was useless.

Annie Eggbaum had been pestering him for months to give up certain secrets about how to get to the end of a novel, and such interactions generally ended in a quiet place hidden from others' eyes, in absolute discretion; but this time the scenario seemed more complicated. He started walking again. The memory of Myriam astride him in the Fiat—although he'd indulged in the same activity several other times without reaching any kind of sexual zenith—returned, flooding his mind at regular intervals, always with the same force. What was he supposed to do about it, he asked himself as he headed back to the house; what was he supposed to do about that meteorite landing in his backyard? Trying to make a joke out of it didn't work any better.

When he got back, he was almost flattened by a heart attack: Myriam was in the living room with his sister, having a cup of coffee, and his sister was saying, "Well, well, here he is, aren't you lucky, here he is; it could have taken a lot more time. Right, Marc?"

He pulled up a chair.

"You're not saying anything. Say something," said Marianne.

"This is Barbara's stepmother."

"I know. We've met."

"I told you about her."

Myriam pushed several notebooks toward him. "I found these," she said. "Wanted to show them to you. But I understand how abrupt this visit is. I'm embarrassed, but I didn't have your telephone number."

He and his sister exchanged glances, then he leaned forward to pick up the notebooks, put on his glasses, and paged through them for a moment—more involved in calming down than in assessing Barbara's work, even if it was as interesting as her stepmother claimed. He wondered whether his forehead was shiny, whether his smiles were turning into grimaces, whether they could tell how embarrassed he was by Myriam's visit.

"Can't wait to read it all," he said. "It's really very kind of you."

He couldn't look into her eyes. It was almost impossible for him. Outside the sun had passed behind the horizon; crows wheeled above the forest.

Suddenly she stood up. Thanked Marianne for the coffee. He lowered his eyes to the notebooks. "I'm going to read all of this," he muttered, caressing them quietly. "It certainly is kind of you."

"Take your time," she said. "No hurry." She drew back toward the door. Marianne hadn't gotten up to accompany her, and nothing could have made him get up out of the chair he was glued to.

He heard the door closing. For several seconds, the silence seemed to vibrate throughout the room. Then she got into her car and the motor droned, before the sound disappeared altogether. Marianne clucked.

"Funny girl. Not educated, but I sense a kind of inner fire, wouldn't you agree?"

"Kind of out of it, if you ask me. You know how much I detest having to deal with students' parents. It's never very healthy."

"Aside from that, what do you think of her?"

He burst out laughing. "You're priceless." He lit a cigarette while she studied him with a smile. Then he looked at his watch. "We're leaving in a half hour," he announced.

"I'm okay. I feel fine."

"A half hour," he repeated. "Don't procrastinate. I'll tell you when I think you're ready to drive again. For today, it's out of the question. Not until you get your strength back. I'll come get you at noon."

"Anyway, the two of you don't seem too at ease with each other."

"You didn't think her busting in like that was annoying? I did. I hope she won't give other people any bad ideas about showing up here the minute their offspring puts ink to paper. Especially at the crack of dawn. Am I attracted to her? Is that what you want to know? Is that the question?"

She made an about-face and headed toward her room. He followed her, stopping on the threshold.

"Your suspicions are becoming unbearable," he sighed. "I'd like to see you in that situation, with a stepdaughter who's disappeared and a husband in the war. I'd like to see you not looking for a little comforting, a few words of conversation with someone else to keep from feeling too alone. Can't you make an effort to understand? Have some empathy? Let go of your fixed ideas? Marianne?"

She was in her slip, leaning over a dresser drawer. The day he'd surprised his mother wearing one, she'd grabbed him by the throat and forced him to turn round and go back all the way to the entrance to the house, then flung him outside, even though he was in his pajamas and was only eight and the north wind threatened to knock him down any second and carry him off like a dry leaf. But it was better than the dark cellar.

———

By noon, he still hadn't seen Myriam again. It wasn't for lack of his having lain in wait for her all morning, going to every building, scouring the cafeteria and vicinity, leaving the door to his office open, etc. The way she'd surprised him a few hours before may have been unsettling, but it had increased his desire to see her again tenfold, to the point that his sister—after studying for a long time the bloody steak he'd ordered for her—asked him if he hadn't been overdoing it on the caffeine, because he seemed unable to stop fidgeting. "It's obvious your mind is somewhere else," she concluded. "How considerate of you."

There was no sense in insisting to the contrary. He was completely aware of his state of mind but couldn't change it, couldn't even give it a name.

A few years before, during a professors' meeting to discuss the behavior of certain students, he'd come down with stomach poisoning and a high fever from eating shellfish—or was it fillet of perch?—and the effects of that fever, as far as he could remember, were a lot like this shaking he felt now, but less severe. It was like stepping into an unknown world, vertigo mixed with dread and irresistible attraction.

"Eat," he told her. "Everything's okay."

"To look at you, I wouldn't say so. You're not eating a thing."

The place was crowded, and the din was just what was needed to prevent all serious conversation and leave him free to keep one eye on the entrances and exits. Ever since she'd literally fled their home early that morning, he'd had a strong desire to say a few words to her, to make up for the halfhearted welcome he'd given her just several hours after the tremendous session she'd accorded him on the roof of the shopping mall.

He didn't know what was happening to him. He needed to take one or two Doliprane®, for lack of better understanding what he was coming down with. One inconvenience of losing your parents too early has to do with being left stranded before learning about life—abandoned midstream. A lot of concepts weren't handed down, a lot of data was missing. A good number of feelings weren't even categorized.

That evening he felt especially depressed. Browbeaten. He hadn't been able to keep his sister company long and had gone upstairs very early to shut himself in his room. Had fallen across the bed with his arms crossed over his chest and stared at the ceiling in the gloomy silence. Seized by a brilliant idea, he pounced on the notebook he'd been carrying with him for years wherever he went, in case something happened. But he'd never managed to do anything good with it until now, nothing that could restore his hope.

He grabbed the pen tucked inside the spirals of the notebook, got ready to write the date, and nothing happened. When still nothing came, he rapidly drew several circles on the paper, but the goddamn pen was out of ink. "Fuck! For God's sake!" he grumbled as he ran all around his room looking for something to write with. Emotion was a rare commodity you had to grab hold of there and then—the stronger the intensity, the shorter the duration. Those were the times you could see what you were worth as a writer, without lying to yourself.

Winded, he glanced at his computer. *I'd sooner die, sooner die*, he thought. But he finally gave in and sat down in front of the screen.

There were several messages. One of them from Myriam. "Are you there?" she was asking. He reread it several times. It had been sent around sunset, about an hour ago. "Hi," he answered. "How are you?"

He got up, went to smoke a cigarette at the window, in the reinvigorating freshness of the starry night. Year after year, the smell of spring tumbling down from the neighboring woods—suddenly hurtling down the hill toward the lake, unimpeded—awed him. *No better cigarette of the day than the one burning here*, he thought, admiring the little beauty he held between his fingers. A light shone on the ground floor, a sign that his sister hadn't gone to bed and might be contemplating the same landscape as he as she smoked. The garden was lit up all the way to the road.

Although the house seemed the same, they'd had the swimming pool resealed, the garden torn up and everything replanted, completely changed, before restoring the grounds; they'd done it so well that today, forty years later, not the slightest trace existed of the events that had occurred. The trees had become big ones, the copses had grown, paths had been designed, a lean-to roof and greenhouse built, and the lawn was kept up from then on. Marc regularly borrowed the electric clippers from the neighbors, and Marianne liked using the pruning shears as a way of fighting depressions. He wondered if Myriam had fallen asleep in front of her screen.

He was so grateful at having these doors unlocked for him, at having had his eyes opened, whatever the result might be. So grateful. He hoped that the angels were watching over her sleep, that her mattress was soft and hand-embroidered. The students could go to the devil from now on. Their blandness could go to the devil. Their pure but distant and insipid flesh could go to the devil, starting today. The target had been shifted upward, toward the heights. There was no looking back.

Annie Eggbaum called, for what it was worth. Her message wasn't very clear because she seemed potted and in a noisy place, but the gist of it was that she was pissed at him, really pissed, and was asking him in quite a loud voice just who he thought he was.

He began by excusing himself, then sent her about her business because she obviously didn't want to listen to him.

Richard called him in two days later and made it clear that he'd crossed a line.

"It was the thing not to do, and you did it," he said in an admiring tone. "I take my hat off to you, really. I congratulate you."

"I didn't touch her."

Richard squealed as if he'd pinched a finger in a door. "I should think not. Oh shit, I should think not. You know who Annie Eggbaum's father is? Jeez, old man. Do you know who Tony Soprano is?" On top of all that, generous donors could be counted on the fingers of one hand. "But I warned you, didn't I buddy? Didn't I tell you to proceed with caution? We don't want any trouble here. You know the situation. Our budgets are getting smaller by the day. This is a record crisis we're in. Listen, I'm about to tell you something that isn't going to feel so good. Old man, this time you've left me no choice."

Marianne got him out of this tight spot. He didn't know exactly how far she'd gone, but she stopped speaking to him and for several days went to lengths to avoid looking at him, refused to share meals with him, ride in his car, without giving him any more explanation. Richard Olso, for his part, pasted a satisfied expression on his face.

"Now, stay out of sight, you hear me? Old man, this is your final warning. Read my lips. Your final warning, okay?"

Nobody wanted to be left at the side of the road in the current climate. It was still too chilly out there. With all the chinks in his armor, it was better to think twice about too much swagger. He nodded. He hadn't done anything, but he knew what kind of opposition he was facing—Richard did too. He lowered his head and left without a word.

But that wasn't all. No sooner had he gotten out of that mess when he was attacked in the parking lot, at the end of the day, as he was leaving Martinelli's office totally lost in thought about how flimsy and insignificant their grievances against him were. All of it was proving to be so disgusting. *With today's unemployment rate reaching new heights, frankly, what could you do with your pride?* he was wondering when a violent blow to his head knocked him to the ground.

There hadn't been any message. The two guys who'd given him the thrashing and knocked him out hadn't said a word. But he didn't need to wrack his brain for hours to find out who this present was from. When he could stand up again and get hold of his handkerchief to sponge up the blood running from his nose, he dragged himself to a pharmacy, dropped onto a chair, and put himself in the hands of a young homosexual in a smock with a disapproving look. He had a clawed cheek, lips as swollen as frankfurters, hands covered with black-and-blue bruises from the blows he'd received while protecting his crotch, disheveled hair, shortness of breath—all of it looked like it was from a particularly violent catfight.

77

Philippe Djian

When he felt better, he thanked the young pharmacist and went back to the parking lot with a gel ice pack pressed to the side of his face, which smarted the most at that moment, eventually changing to the other cheek.

The Eggbaums seemed to be genuine maniacs. Father and daughter. He studied himself in the rearview mirror, grimacing because of his ribs. But this wasn't the first thrashing in his life he'd received, and he almost smiled after verifying that he still had all his teeth—especially the three outrageously expensive implants Marianne had generously paid for on his fiftieth birthday. Basically, he'd gotten off easy. It was clear that these people didn't play by the rules.

Nor was it the first time Marianne had seen him in such a state. How many ice packs had she brought for him, how many bandages had she applied, and how many aspirins had she given him to take since the time they were old enough to stand up?

"So, you're running after that girl?" she said in a neutral tone.

"I refused to tutor her privately. She's the one who was running after me. I hope you can grasp that slight difference."

Because she was leaning over his cuts and bumps, he automatically had a direct view of her personal charms, was able to see down the inside of her apple-green kimono. Under normal circumstances it was enough to make him nervous, to force him to leave and get a little fresh air. By nature, their relationship was rarely simple. Obviously, nothing was very clear. Very early, they'd had to hold each other tight, touch, hug, caress, in order to rein in their fears, smother their sobs, clinging to each other as long as the storm lasted or they'd been sent to their rooms without eating. As a little girl, Marianne cried a lot, preferably in the hollow of his shoulder; and then, heartsick, he had to go and

78

change his clothes, looking as if somebody had thrown a bowl of briny water onto his chest.

Her tears were tepid and salty. He knew the smell of her perspiration and hair and other odors, which sometimes hit him like lightning; but seeing her chest that evening, a sight that would have normally made him tremble like the frailest leaf, glimpsing her pear-shaped breasts, their tips, left him cold.

Obviously, his physical state had something to do with it. That beating certainly hadn't put him in any kind of raunchy mood, but did that really explain it?

He had himself disinfected, daubed with arnica cream, and then he smoked a cigarette.

He couldn't get over it. Experiencing such a difference. This unexpected void inside him. "What's the matter?" she asked, freezing for a moment. He blinked at her as a way of saying that everything was okay, gave her a faint smile. His forehead and jaw were smarting. Breathing through his nose wasn't easy. His hands were killing him.

But was it the price of peace? Why not, after all? If the Eggbaums considered it even, he was willing to leave it at that. He'd offended Annie Eggbaum and been given a thrashing in return. Fine. And for god's sake, how delicious that cigarette tasted as he surveyed the calm night in the garden.

Of course, Myriam was the cause of this strange phenomenon. Never had any of his youthful conquests prevented him from being ultrareactive to bodies, and to his sister's physical presence. Never had any of his friendly students gratified him to the point of feeling what he'd felt for Marianne today; nothing at all, in fact, as improbable as it was—at least from a strictly carnal point of view.

God knows, that green kimono had fed a host of fantasies. At times, just the sight of it, even when it was hanging in the closet on a soulless hanger, floored him. Some girls had noticed how heavily chained he was to his relationship with his sister—and although his affairs with these girls now seemed like nothing but seven-day wonders, he had to admit they had a certain intuition and were right. But knowing this was like looking directly at the sun at high noon; he was blinded immediately, couldn't say a word, was incapable of describing what he was feeling.

Was it all in the past? Whatever the case, getting Annie Eggbaum out of the game wasn't any less the healthy and only attitude to adopt, to avoid being plunged into inextricable chaos. He ran the tip of his tongue over his throbbing lips and noticed Marianne looking at him.

"I'm not the unhinged person you think I am," he sighed. "I didn't have an affair with that student. But this guy, he's Tony Soprano. You know who Tony Soprano is? No? Well, don't think you're living in a civilized country. Most people are still living like they did in the Dark Ages."

"And meanwhile, I've been sacrificing for you. To keep you from being given the boot. I sacrifice for you, and this is the reward I get. Well, that'll teach me, won't it?"

She was among the last women in the world who smoked Gitanes. And when she exhaled the smoke in your face, everything around you disappeared in an awful fog. "Good night," she said, turning on her heels.

At least, he thought, *she is starting to talk to me again.*

Now he realized he'd been very hard on her. Before the time he'd placed a hand on a woman, and before he'd admitted he'd never be anything but a mediocre writer, he'd been vicious. But after he'd tried one out and accepted the latter, his mind calmed down a great deal, his mood softened. His conduct adopted a less brutal, less exacting, less negative tone; but it was a bit late to offer Marianne the smile that she'd probably always been without.

Even so, he wanted to protect her. As much as possible. Keep her safe. He certainly owed her that. He gave several little knocks on the door of her room to wish her good night as he walked by. She was crying. He hated to hear her cry. It was something he couldn't stand. So he retraced his steps and put on his coat and left the house. Outside, the moon sparkled in the sky like a diamond in its case—literally. It was cold. He lit a cigarette and walked through the garden until he got to the road, which a light, low cloud of fog was beginning to cover.

He walked through it, plunged into the woods.

*In the morning, he woke up in the Fiat, feeling terribly moth-*eaten and frozen stiff. The water vapor condensed on the windshield formed a network of tiny silver rivers. He studied them for a moment before deciding to budge. The sun had barely risen.

How had he landed there? Weird. What had he been up to during the entire night? He noticed the mud coating his shoes, drying on the cuffs of his pants and on his coat. His hands were dirty. His legs exhausted—but pleased. Apparently the jaunt had been long, athletic.

Hard to know what passed through his mind from time to time. In all honesty, he wasn't too sure of it himself; his only certainty, for the moment, was that he was dying of hunger.

He opened the car door, stuck out one leg, then the other, then an arm into the golden sunshine spreading through the garden in a flurry of light, telling himself that a half-dozen eggs was just what he needed. Once outside, he stretched and stared at the expanse of azure, yawning his head off. It was quickly becoming a clear morning, the light banishing shadows. Sparrows were perched on the electric wires waiting for the rays of the sun to plump up their feathers, save them from the icy embrace of night.

Not a sound in the house. He hung his cap and coat at the entrance, then immediately headed for the fridge. When she was feeling in good enough shape, Marianne changed to twenty-percent fat content, which was nearly edible, but the zero-percent was really revolting, incredibly depressing, despicably repellent. Despite this, he took the top off a jar of the vanilla-flavored stuff and served himself some before tackling whatever else there was.

This type of exercise—these long, random walks—gave him an appetite for almost the entire day. Marianne thought he was somewhat of a sleepwalker; and although she didn't much appreciate knowing he was wandering outside the entire night—exactly where, no one really knew—she saw no point in giving the phenomenon more importance than it had, in her opinion. At the very most, she'd made him put up with a few acupuncture sessions to ease her conscience, or sent him for treatment by hypnosis; but there was nothing very conclusive about any of it, no tangible results.

He found eggs. A dog barked in the distance as the sun suddenly loomed above the woods. No bacon or ham, of course—Marianne had stopped doing any grocery shopping for almost a month. He looked down and swore to take care of it, found some frozen croissants, checked his watch. There was still enough time to place an order. He ought to buy some steaks, rib steaks, a whole joint of roast beef, all kinds of meat—except horse meat—if he wanted her to recover and get back some color.

For a moment he watched the eggs cooking, then looked up and straight ahead toward the garden, blazing with sunlight. He'd covered quite a distance; that was about all he could say about it. His appetite afterward. The smell of the woods clinging to him, the odor of damp earth and dead leaves. Stone, sap, and resin. That's all he could say about it.

When suddenly, as the eggs sizzled in the pan, Myriam loomed up before him, on the other side of the window, like a jack-in-the-box devil.

After a second of hesitation, he turned off the gas and signaled to her that he was coming. As he went toward her, a mild case of pins and needles ran through his entire body, and his mouth became dry—just as had happened at the end of the sixties when he'd take acid. No student affected him that way. He never knew where he was headed when it came to her. It was as simple as that. Toward dry land, even inhabited land? How could he know? What were the ground rules? What parts of it were comparable? He and his sister hadn't had a great deal of experience in the world around them, he admitted, but had anyone ever heard him claiming they had?

She was waiting near her car. He was holding a still-frozen croissant, he suddenly realized, but since it was too late to get rid of it discreetly, he didn't and could feel his fingers numbing as she headed resolutely toward him.

The words began rushing to his lips as he watched her approach, bolting toward him, even, when she was only a few feet away. Then he was pinned against the wall, with Myriam's lips glued to his, their tongues penetrating each other's mouths, their bodies tightly melded, before he'd had the time to say *whew*. And the dog in the distance kept howling—there'd been an increase in the number of stray dogs as the price of dog food went up and real estate went down.

Sensational. There wasn't any other word. Absolutely sensational, this kiss she was treating him to on the doorstep, without having said a single word. Undeniably delightful. He threw the croissant into the bushes and pressed her to him, closing his eyes.

When he opened them again, feeling totally dazed, ecstatic, his hands empty and his breath short, his back pressed firmly to the wall, he saw her climbing back into her car, with still no explanation, starting the motor, and disappearing as quickly as she'd come.

He stayed there unmoving for a few minutes, close to panting, as the sound of the motor was gradually lost in the morning mist. The wisteria framing the entranceway filled the air with its strong fragrance. He went back to eat his eggs, but there was no reason any longer to hurry for things like that.

There was no doubt about it; her rhythms were going to drive him out of his mind, he told himself, offering a vague smile to the entranceway mirror.

This time, he would have liked to talk it all over with Marianne. He'd never felt the need before. He would have been interested in her interpretation of the strangely intense kiss he'd just received, what meaning it could have, what she thought of it, what she thought he should do about it, etc.—even her advice would have been welcome. Unfortunately, it was impossible, he had to give up that idea. His sister wasn't ready.

"What happened?" she said. "I heard some noise."

She looked disheveled, barely awake. He stirred the eggs he'd put back on the stove, but which he didn't feel like having anymore. "No, you dreamed it," he replied. "Must have been the radio. Have a seat. I made some eggs for you. You dreamed it all."

She snickered, but had no proof of what she was about to put forward. "And how is it that you're already up?" she muttered, frowning. She studied him for a moment and then opened her mouth, but no sound came out. He shrugged to express his helplessness, to tell her that there were certain things you were never even close to getting over.

At the end of the morning he'd asked his students to write one page about the things that went through their minds during the next half hour. As a whole, the results weren't very spectacular. Such slim pickings left him perplexed. The forces of creativity certainly weren't in evidence that morning; many students hadn't even woken up, or felt abused by such a totally impromptu exercise, which seemed especially stressful the day after a weekend. As he was leaving class and closing his briefcase, a pencil still stuck between his teeth, he was pulled aside by their union representative—known for the courses he gave on universities of the late Middle Ages—and told what had been brewing behind his back. The man had been following all these developments with a magnifying glass and since spring 2007 had had nothing to report but bad news.

Putting it simply, his writing workshop was finished. They were putting an end to the post. Those of two other teachers as well. New economical measures would be put in place continually, in one way or another. We need to hold up in the face of all opposition, the representative would drone, nodding his head all the while, without anyone really understanding what he was talking about. "In my entire working career, I've never seen such a shambles," the union man went on. "We need to face it head on. It's a question of survival."

Marc made a vague gesture of agreement and took the cigarette offered by the union guy, who let out a soul-rending sigh and added, "Go ahead. Take two."

Once he was alone, he went and sat on a bench next to the red-brick buildings that contained the library on one side and the administration on the other, which was where Marianne worked. Maybe he didn't want to speak to her right away, but he felt better knowing she was nearby if he needed to. He wasn't the only person who'd been undermined by losing a job, and he wasn't so sure he'd react more intelligently to such a situation than any of them had.

There still are some people who smoke those filthy Marlboros, he thought, lighting the one he'd tucked behind his ear as he was finding out he'd been given the boot, realizing that Richard and Martinelli had finally agreed to can him, kick him out without any consideration, apart from that for the school system.

Did it mean that Marianne had given in to Richard Olso's sexual cravings? Had the bastard tricked her to such an extent? That simple thought gave him a migraine. It was sunny today, but not too hot. In his current state, with his brain boiling, too big a dose of sun would have laid him flat on the spot.

How could she have been stupid enough to trust such a shyster? What was she hoping for when she did?

"Didn't I tell you? I certainly told you it was a mistake."

She'd sat down next to him on the bench right after getting his message. Her neck had sunk between her shoulders, and on both sides her hands gripped the bench, her eyes staring straight ahead. "That-god-damn-cre-tin," he said, without raising his voice, enunciating each syllable as he shook his head resignedly. He slapped his thighs. "I hope you gave him the reward he deserved."

Night was beginning to fall. The few hours since he'd been fired had gone by in the blink of an eye. He hadn't even been aware of it.

"What is it you want to say, exactly?" she answered, her tone dismal.

There was a sandwich in front of him. He hadn't eaten anything since morning. He shrugged. "It's not important, is it? What's done is done."

Her head turned away toward the setting sun, as its last gleams touched the stained-glass windows in the library. "I didn't sleep with him," she declared.

He leaped to his feet. "Oh, please! Spare me the details!" he exploded, striding back and forth, his fists stuck in his pockets. "Keep them to yourself, will you? Do me the favor. But he certainly did fuck with you, your little boyfriend, he really took you for a ride, as they say."

Once again, she stopped speaking to him for several days, and as a result the house was turned into a cold, silent tomb. He took advantage of it to think about his current situation and to watch a few movies in the living room as soon as she left to go to work—and she never opened her mouth.

When she came home in the evening, she denied him the slightest glance and completely ignored him as she went from room to room taking care of things. She had a nasty temper that wasn't about to improve. Aging was starting to get scary, when you thought about it.

"I don't need your gratitude," she wrote to him on a measly scrap of paper. He'd been to see Martinelli in person, and that asshole of a president had announced in a jolly tone—almost getting a kick out of the joke—that he'd been granted a stay of execution. It was because most of the teachers had gotten emotional about it, especially Richard Olso, who'd become his most fervent defender. Pure magic. His darling sister. He wanted to thank her for the trouble she'd gone to yet again, tell her that he hadn't been taken in by this sudden reversal credited to Richard. However, given the atmosphere that her loathsome silence had established, he'd have to put off his overtures of friendship until later, when she'd be able to listen to them.

How did she do it? What potion was she using? How was she managing to get what she wanted? If she wasn't sleeping with him, how was she rewarding him? This simple question made him shudder. Not that he thought that she hadn't been involved with anyone all these years, that she was some kind of virgin who'd gotten a little nutty after fifty years of abstinence. But with Richard Olso, the context, the mode, were different. This wasn't a man she'd met in a bar or ran into at a party. It was the man who'd swiped the keys to the literature department from him. The guy who knew almost nothing, had practically no ear, found no thrill in the magic of balance; a type from another age. He was a worshipper of a few old Goncourt authors nobody remembered, some starchy poets and atrocious new talents; a miserable reader, in any case, somebody who never had a clue and was always on the wrong track. How could anyone be that blind to the light, so impoverished inside? It was staggering. Absolutely staggering.

Thinking of the various attentions that Richard Olso had managed to get from Marianne, even if she didn't call it "sleeping with him," disturbed him, hurt him deeply for all these reasons—and being the cause of it didn't help matters.

Whatever the case, he'd now been spared from giving up his office, and that was something. The coming chaos he'd been dreading, the thought of total disorder that turned him pale in advance, the disruption of his 100-square-foot space—not to mention his view of the lake through eucalyptus trees and a part of the faraway snow-covered Alps that he'd almost come to believe as belonging to him—fortunately hadn't happened. The alert had been lifted. He sent an e-mail to his students to inform them that their venerable university had reinstated him and asked them to dive into Nabokov and study each page carefully without being given any other explanation, unless they had doubts about the notion of precision, the mechanics of clock-making. Then he gave himself a few extra days off to make up for the stress caused by his loss of employment.

In the mornings, as soon as the sun rose, the temperature climbed, and you could be outdoors with a sweater and a good scarf.

Thinking of Myriam set off a kind of pang that could go on for a good part of the day. Deciding to watch a Ben Stiller movie promised to bring some respite. Until he started trying to find it and lost interest in the idea. It had been about a week since their kiss, but every moment since had lasted an eternity.

He went back to his classes, then slipped away at the end of the afternoon to go directly to her place.

He smoked a cigarette on the sidewalk opposite. Later he smoked another lying next to her in the darkness of the bedroom; this didn't bother her. She herself smoked in bed sometimes, she said. He touched her temple, to which perspiration had glued some locks of her hair. She was slender, almost scrawny, but it excited him. Firm, pointed breasts, white and pink.

He rose without a word, got dressed in a kind of trance. The day was starting to filter through the drawn curtains. She opened her eyes but didn't move, studied the way he carefully restyled his hair, put on his undershorts, stretched his neck—a total zombie. In the doorway he turned around and gestured to her, but God knew what he was really looking at. The eyes were empty.

Back on the street he still felt drowsy, calm. When he looked up, he noticed something behind her window—a statue of the Virgin illuminated with a candle, scarily beautiful. He hurried.

The girl in the cafeteria let him in. He offered her a cigarette. There were no customers yet. On the terrace outside, the tables were covered with dew, their umbrellas glistening. The sky was turning blue. Newspapers were spread across the counter of the bar—the end of the world was close—something nobody doubted anymore with all the proofs accumulating, so much inevitability already established. Anyway, his horoscope was favorable, indicating an upswing. An encounter wasn't impossible. Open your eyes. Usually, he avoided pastries and sugary tarts, but he needed to get his strength back while his eggs were sizzling in the kitchen and the bread was toasting. He reached for the croissants while still bent over an article about the basic precautions to take in case of a nuclear attack, based on the premise of the local plant or even an army laboratory exploding into smithereens. Stay shut up at home. Don't move. Wait for help to come. Don't take any initiative. Dial 112, the emergency telephone number, etc.

Instead of closing on a croissant, which was probably just the right temperature this time, it was another hand, some fingers, belonging to the detective investigating Barbara's disappearance. The same one, he realized, raising his eyes to the young guy, who stunk of aftershave and confidently offered him (in spite of the forced, artificial quality of the result) his most charming, taken-aback smile.

Both of them politely apologized for their mutual blunder; according to the detective, he'd been distracted by reading his text messages.

They agreed that it was going to be a lovely day. He'd served himself first, figuring that because he was older he had the right of way; and at present he was dunking the end of his croissant in his coffee, wondering whether he'd be able to leave the counter to sit down at a table and eat breakfast in peace. But you had to keep in mind that this guy was a police officer, and nobody wanted the complications of irking one, today more than ever, with all the flouting of civil rights; not to mention all the people you had to deal with, all of them so touchy and quick to take offense, completely ready to throw you into the back of some cell on the slightest pretext.

Prison represented the worst nightmare you could imagine. Whenever he thought about it, he liked to be sitting down, since he got short of breath. He imagined getting hold of cyanide capsules and keeping them under his tongue, in case he was ever threatened with getting locked up. Just the thought of it took his breath away. And who'd take care of Marianne if he disappeared? Who'd look after her?

He didn't feel very fresh in yesterday's clothing, hadn't washed or shaved, so he refrained from making too bad an impression by refolding his newspaper and paying some attention to the man, presently holding forth on the weather for the next six days. Captivating subject—or at least one that tempted you to take off for the Caribbean at the last minute (the fare happened to be on sale for two hundred euros).

The detective looked around thirty. Kind of plump. From the way he sounded, it wasn't from the croissants—he'd given up smoking. Drinking, too, maybe. Or else his wife was cooking a little too much for him, he joked. "You never can trust women, right?"

"You said it, Inspector. Hearing you loud and clear."

He was dying to ask the detective about his reasons for being in the campus cafeteria so early in the morning, but he kept his mouth shut. He wasn't going to make the slightest mistake. When the eggs arrived, he looked up and smiled at the waitress.

"You're a teacher, right, and a very early riser?" observed the detective, eyeing his fried eggs.

"No, this is an exception," he answered, "a happy one. Or I wouldn't be able to handle it."

He had to keep staring at the detective for a good fifteen seconds before the other understood and nodded with a smile, saying, "Sorry, I didn't want to pry."

"You're not prying, Inspector. Believe me, the fact you were doing your job doesn't shock me. It's obvious crime's on the rise in this country."

The detective signaled the waitress to let her know that he wanted the same thing, fried eggs. At this point the place had filled up; two new girls had begun working, and a second cook had gone into the kitchen.

The detective was there on a campus drug case, but he hadn't forgotten about Barbara's disappearance. "Spoke to her step-mother the other day. Promised her we were doing our best, but what can we do? We don't have a body, don't have anything. And it's a wide, wide world, you know."

He agreed with the officer, who was now intently giving him the once-over.

"Did you fall down the stairs?" the man asked. "You don't have to answer. This isn't an interrogation."

"No, not the stairs. Does it look that nasty?"

"No . . . Just a little yellow. Blue. Your lip is split a little."

"A little? Listen, some guys jumped me the other night. They attacked me in the parking lot, bashed my head in. Don't ask me why. Who even knows if there was a reason. Nowadays, people get stabbed right in the middle of the street for next to nothing, but I don't have to tell you that. Useless to go looking for an answer to everything. As a whole, people are getting nuttier and nuttier. Right? Don't you think so? Anyway, they really worked me over."

"Know what you mean. We're up to here with it. Sorry about it. But it's becoming unmanageable. Evil's out of hand in this country. If you can't even make it from your office to your car without getting beat up by the neighborhood loonies, things aren't working anymore, they've gone kerflooey. What do you think they wanted?"

"Beats me!"

This time, just as he was saying the word *beats*, he spotted her at the entrance, unmoving, pale, her hair a mess, her eyes trained on him. A few hours ago, he'd still been holding this woman in his arms, both of them relentlessly engaged in every kind of intimate caress until daybreak, and he'd taken her in all kinds of positions until they were both completely exhausted and came for the last time around five in the morning. Sated, wiped out. But apparently, it wasn't enough. It hadn't prevented a thing, to judge from the violent desire taking possession of him once more. His appetite for her rewhetted like a razor, burst forth again like a flame from an ember in a burning blast. It made him jump to his feet and put a bill on the counter without waiting for his change or offering the detective a word of excuse. Without the slightest discretion appropriate for such a situation, he walked straight toward her in broad daylight, scorned again every rule that had been imposed on him, pushed those in the way aside, and went straight for her. In public. Right under the nose of the detective, who was watching the whole thing with unconcealed interest.

This time the encounter took place in the red-brick building next door, which contained the library and a carefully remodeled multipurpose auditorium with ultramodern equipment, and which had toilets the students could not access. He steered her along. Didn't feel very comfortable with the idea that he was taking her somewhere he'd used two or three times before, for nearly identical reasons; but right now he was devoured by desire, nothing else counted.

The funniest thing was that he'd anticipated this possibility, pictured it countless times, mentally prepared himself to face it and firmly resist it. Now here he was succumbing at the first bout, losing all control—and as a result, any way of protecting himself. Here he was leading Myriam to the toilets.

After walking through her door the evening before, no more than a minute had gone by before he began making love to her, after a long kiss that had made his head spin. That meant they'd barely had a chance to exchange more than a few words since they'd become lovers, if he added it all up.

And here it came again. As if they grew speechless the moment they found themselves face to face. They tore down the stairs leading to the stage, then branched off toward the washbasins, without a single word. Never. Never. Never would he have believed that desire this consuming could exist, that it could swallow him up to this extent. They didn't go there; they ran. Like a couple of high school students, crazed, insatiable young dogs. Some miracle kept them from running into anyone else, such as a cleaning lady with her pail or a stray electrician.

While he gasped for air, she put a hand on his shoulder and used the time to pull off her panties, hopping from one leg to the other. Then she hitched up her skirt.

He couldn't wait to be able to invite her to lunch. He wanted to get to know her, discover who she was, what kind of book she was reading, and blah-blah-blah-talk with her and tell her in a low voice how new this was for him, how excited he was by this new continent, this astounding virgin territory that she was opening up to him; but obviously that wasn't going to happen tomorrow. This was no pleasure cruise that encouraged chatting.

Clearly, proof of patience was necessary in this context. You had to accept these silent encounters, which could, moreover, prove to be the sign of an adult relationship, the kind you strike up with mature women and not with young girls, a sign of that milestone you pass on your path to deserving the older ones, becoming appreciated by them and invited into their game, assuming the position of a worthy partner. Maybe silence was indispensable to such ventures at the beginning. Maybe you had to see it as the fly that hovers over the truffle, the sign of a serious affair that certainly was getting off to an auspicious start.

When they were done, they listened to each other's breathing. It always felt good coming back to life. Then they tidied up their clothing. Washed their hands. Glanced at each other silently in the mirror as they were drying them. Deep inside, he was laughing at the thought of the two or three students he'd taken here. What a journey he'd made today, what a leap forward. At the height of the experience, hadn't he let out a slight moan and then trembled for almost a minute against her after he'd ejaculated? Had he ever known anything like it? Deep down, he was little more than a child. He admitted it. He'd known nothing about it before today. He'd been born today. He remembered that one of his past conquests had had a weakness for lavatories, the smell, something he'd thought of as the last word when it came to sexual maturity. He chuckled to himself silently.

He pitied the man he'd been until now, the poverty of his existence. With a slight shrug he lit a cigarette. Asked her if she wanted one. She accepted. He said he'd be happy to buy her a coffee. She accepted. He nodded.

They went back to the cafeteria—he actually gave a start when their fingers brushed against each other as they walked, which at least made her laugh. The sun was getting stronger, and soon it would surge up over the crests. The students they passed still had sleepy faces. The grass was still damp, and the tongue of mist unraveling on the lake seemed the result of some mysterious, languid molting that had fallen to Earth during the night.

Together they walked into the room. Frankly, he knew no better way of attracting all kinds of trouble. It was pure rapture.

The next day, Richard Olso explained to him how badly viewed were a certain professor's too friendly relations with the step-mother of a student who'd disappeared—little Barbara, about whom there was still no news.

He listened silently, wondering how such things could be possible. Sometimes, when he thought about Richard Olso, when he examined him from head to toe, as he was at that moment, and stared at his ugly face and ridiculous goatee, all the merit of Marianne's sacrifice stood out. The poor girl. The poor girl. On the other hand, he'd never asked for anything of the sort. He would have never been able to ask for such a thing. No one had asked her for anything. He couldn't assume such a burden. Not that one. Out of the question. Besides, she herself wasn't very clear about it. She could never look him in the eyes when he brought it up. She'd never formally admitted that she disliked Richard, not really, not one single time; there was that two-faced way she had when she said, no, not at all, adamantly shaking her head, even though it was as plain as the nose on her face, even though, obviously, she was far from being impervious to the interest he showed in her.

Richard Olso was complaining that he wasn't listening. "Listen to me, old man. Soon I won't know any more how to handle you, you know. Marianne knows it. I won't always be able to intervene. But what's up with your hanging around that woman? Are you doing it on purpose, or what? I mean, she's the only one you can find? Are you sure you've really looked around?" In the middle of the black ocean made up of being fired from work, a spot of light was forming, and this pool of light came from a feeling of freedom regained, no longer having to put up with any kind of oppression, wherever it came from; no longer having anybody over him. Being outside the realm of the All-Powerful. Too bad he hadn't been fired and that Richard Olso was still his superior.

At any rate, he didn't intend to bring this relationship into the light of day. He knew the cafeteria episode wasn't an example of any very clever or responsible behavior on his part. Carrying on with her in public. Practically being seen on her arm. He. A man in his situation. Not that he regretted that act of bravado. Absolutely not. He'd savored every second, every minute of it; but he couldn't allow himself to play around with his security. That was a luxury he couldn't afford.

He had to restore the protections around him. "All right, Richard, I'll make you a promise. You won't hear any more about this business. I promise you total discretion. No meetings on campus nor anywhere near it. No stir. No making waves. How's that?"

"Marc, I'm not your enemy. Do you know that?"

Philippe Djian

"Any man who's hanging around my sister is my enemy. Just joking."

"We could hit it off, you and me. But that doesn't seem to occur to you."

"It doesn't? Really?"

"I'm having a barbecue Sunday. Are you coming?"

"Are you asking if I'd come to your barbecue?"

"Yes, exactly."

"Sunday? This Sunday?"

When he spoke about it to Marianne, she suddenly seemed to recover her speech, and questioned him about the rumor about him and that woman.

"Don't listen to gossip," he told her. "I haven't done anything but drink coffee with her. It's okay. That shouldn't send me to hell. It's okay. Let's not start up again."

"A bit too easy an answer, isn't it?"

"It has nothing to do with being easy or not. It has to do with refusing to argue when there are no grounds for it."

"Argue? About what? I don't give a good goddamn about you and your whore."

With those words, she guffawed. He handed her a glass of white wine and turned toward the sunset, which was powdering the horizon orangish. Gossip traveled quickly, spread almost instantaneously. Their foray to the toilets in the multipurpose auditorium and the robust breakfast that followed—they'd helped themselves to a basket of fresh croissants as they waited for the eggs and waffles they'd ordered—had only happened yesterday, but the campus rumor about a creative writing professor going out with the wife of a soldier who'd been sent to Afghanistan was already on everybody's lips.

100

He was in a good position to know what Marianne was feeling since he'd experienced it a hundred times himself, that fear of being abandoned, that horrible fear of being abandoned, with nothing that could save you. But he was the boy, despite the fact that she was older; he was the boy who had to set the example, even if it meant clenching his teeth a little harder when problems arrived—and he'd never hesitated, not as long as their mother had run things.

Of course, he had no intention of failing in his role with regards to his sister. His own health depended on it. Hadn't he spared her from his past adventures to a large extent? Hadn't he demonstrated that he was the most discreet of men? Had he given her any serious reason to see her position as threatened?

He sat down near her and massaged her feet. He was largely persuaded that he shouldn't change any of that, that they'd miraculously succeeded in achieving a kind of equilibrium—but what an equilibrium, what a monstrous one. So much fragility was mind-boggling. So much weakness disconcerting. Few people had figured that brother and sister would somehow regain their footing one day. Taking into account the path they'd traveled, the fact that they were where they were today made those who knew the story respect them.

How could he ever cancel all that out? Moments like this. Weren't they living what they'd promised each other during their most intense ordeals? Hadn't they finally found peace, satisfaction, freedom, everything they'd ever wanted, ever strived for?

"Everything is fine," he said.

"Obviously everything is not fine. Nobody's forcing you to say anything at all, it's really irritating."

He put Marianne's feet back down and lit a cigarette. Last

year they'd put a nice sum into this top-of-the-line couch, which was unbelievably comfortable and spacious—some creep had been crazy enough to push up the bidding, but they'd held out, had finally outbid the son-of-a-bitch around three in the morning and become the owners of this folly for around ten times the price of a normal couch. But they hadn't regretted it for an instant, nor the way they found each of their beddings, choosing carefully after visiting nearly every online shop on the planet. He remembered how excited they were at the idea of each of them possessing his or her own bed, sheets and pillowcases, and the blankets that went with them. He leaned back, thinking that you had to have slept on the ground for a long time, even on the floor for years, before you could fully appreciate the quality of the seat on which he was sitting.

He'd ended up there one evening with a student—they'd taken advantage of a wildcat strike paralyzing the entire country and keeping Marianne at the far end of the province for the night; and the experience had been conclusive. What a piece of furniture was stuffed with didn't count for everything. Besides the quality of the springs and the density of the foam, which were both excellent, contact with the leather upholstery—a magnificent kid leather that was thick, supple, and arousing—made for everything, according to the student, and based on the small amount of time they lay there naked and kind of carefully wriggled their butts on it.

"Listen," he said to her. She stopped studying her toes and looked up. "Now listen closely. In the first place, you have nothing to worry about and you never will from me. I didn't think I needed to remind you of that. You can sleep soundly. You're my sister, I love you. On the one hand. Now, excuse me, but, on the other hand, allow me to point out to you, that I, for one, am not making a big deal about your relationship with that idiot. Do you really think I get a kick out of seeing you go out with that . . ."

"Go out?"

"Please, Marianne. What difference does it make what name you give it? I mean, shit, call it what you want. And in any case, I'm not going to his barbecue. I'm not going to eat sausages and get smoked in his backyard. I wouldn't count on it. You can do your thing with him in peace. Thank me."

She grabbed a pitiful little statuette that happened to be in reach and smashed it on the floor, where it shattered into a thousand pieces.

It was a statue of the Blessed Virgin that changed color over time, like the hundreds of thousands like it being sold at Lourdes. It was night now. Their father had often encouraged their mother to break a dish rather than swallow her anger, but she had seldom resorted to that, and the results were well known.

At least Marianne was breaking something, and he associated the sound of glass, or smashed porcelain, anything broken into bits, with release, not the thunder that comes before a storm but that which suddenly stops the rain and brings back a blue sky, and silence.

He himself preferred walking—fast, through the woods—and the yelling that welled up when he figured he was far enough away, alone; it was a roar that would spring up out of him like the flow of blood from a big, wounded animal. Everyone had his method. His mother, as well, was the type who screamed, wrung her hands, rolled around on the floor, tore out her hair. Whole patches of it. Sometimes to the point where it looked like she'd caught ringworm.

For a long time he'd wondered if the Virgin's change in color should have been considered a miracle, or at least hypothesized to be one; and he thought about the fact that he'd never see her again and realized that he'd become used to glancing that way at least once a day. Until now.

The smallest fragments sparkled like snow on the floor, like powdered sugar. He got up and made a fire while she swept the largest pieces into a dustpan—if you could call it that. He wasn't sorry about having been so blunt with her. It behooved him to take into account, in one way or another, whatever she was accepting from Richard, regardless of the reason. What she would have accepted from anyone at all obviously wouldn't have been very pleasant for him to imagine, either; but Richard Olso was the worst of all. He'd swept her away on all counts, gotten hold of her from start to finish. There should have been a law for sisters like that who were so incredibly good at unearthing the mangiest dog in the entire region, the most pathetic lover for a hundred leagues around, the perfect asshole guaranteed to ruin your life for centuries. There ought to be the harshest of laws. It made more sense having a brother, in every case. Why complicate things?

His brother, the one he was supposed to have had, was born dead—or almost—he'd only survived a few days. This brother was his great regret. This older brother who would have at least shared his burden, made life easier—and kept all that followed from happening, couldn't he have? How many times had he fantasized about it? How many times had he kept an image of this brother with him when he was at his lowest, totally at the mercy of abuse, being humiliated or deprived of food, completely discouraged?

The simple act of thinking of this brother lit up his face with a pleasant smile while flames began dancing on the walls.

Marianne added some more incense. Luckily, his mind was occupied by another woman, because his sister, who'd lain down again on the couch, had revealed a potent sight: a view of the bottom of her ivory-colored satin panties. Luckily, he was thinking solely about another woman while Marianne kept this immodest position, more or less innocently—her long bare legs with their white thighs, her half hiked-up skirt, the soft stream of pungent smoke she was dreamily sending toward the ceiling.

"I know how to get another one," she said.

"Really? What are you talking about?"

"Another Blessed Virgin. All right? I'll buy another one."

"Good. Get two."

*T*he alcohol attracted the students, and Richard had prom- ised them the bar would be well stocked—just as he'd as- sured the teaching body that the food would be good and their not being there unforgivable.

Generally, any department head organizing a party defi- nitely wouldn't be snubbed, but this was even less the case when the president himself was making the trip with his wife and drinking your champagne and wolfing down your mixed grill. Richard's backyard was fairly full. The fellow had the advantage of good spring weather, and his barbecue was roar- ing—at least the guy knew how to cook sausages and chicken breasts.

It was nice out, and the women were wearing sandals. Marc and Marianne made their appearance just as Richard was putting on a new batch of kebabs.

"It's great having you, Marc, and your sister. Hope you know that. Hope there's no misunderstanding here."

"No, everything's cool. What do you suggest? Not too much fat, if possible."

"I've got what you need. Taste this."

"Really?"

"Come on over, Marc. I want to tell you something. Can I confide in you?"

"No, Richard, I'd rather not. I'd rather you say it right out. I don't want to keep a secret from anybody. It's nothing personal. I don't want the responsibility. I sleepwalk. Ask Marianne. I talk while I'm asleep. I walk around talking. It's as simple as that. When it comes to anything confidential, old buddy, I'm not the one to go to. I'm not worth a rat's ass when it comes to confidences."

Behind them, several professors were getting a laugh at the sight of a handful of little kids they'd brought and who were grinningly confronting one another with water pistols. Richard smiled, turned over a few ribs.

"Marc, I just wanted to say that I appreciate your coming. You know, I'm aware of the efforts you make. I can put myself in your place. I never had a sister, but I try to put myself in your place."

"How nice of you. Comforting. Anyway, your little party's a big success. You wouldn't happen to have any English mustard, would you?"

A half-dozen students who'd been more or less ordered to come to the party were busy going from one group to another, serving and keeping an eye on those children who'd been given free rein, making sure they weren't going to wreck the inside of the house, turn on the gas, get locked in a closet, or start a fire. Richard knew how to take advantage of his position and hadn't had any problem finding a workforce. Including Annie Eggbaum. Marc didn't notice her until the moment he was pinned against her between two tables as the two of them were passing from opposite directions. For a second they were stuck together.

"Well, Annie, of all people!" he said, keeping his hands in sight.

She gave him a dark look.

A little later, as he was extricating himself from a group who wanted to go all the way to the European Parliament over the issue of the right of Muslim women to wear a veil to school, she put herself in front of him, cheeks red with anger, and asked what the problem was.

In a career of more than twenty years, he'd never seen such behavior, such lack of respect. Such arrogance, insolence. He may have been twice her age, but she was hammering at him unrestrainedly, pushing him against the ropes.

He looked around furtively and asked that she lower her voice.

"What's your problem, huh, tell me!" she said, her temper flaring.

At first he thought he'd definitely have to strangle her to keep her quiet, because not only wasn't she speaking more softly, her voice had reached a shriek. For lack of a better solution, he took her firmly by the elbow and, smiling, led her aside.

"My god, you're insane," he uttered between his teeth. "What's come over you? Is it about that business of lessons? Is that it?"

"You know very well that it's not about that," she hissed back, "so stop playing dumb."

"Excuse me?"

"You understood perfectly."

"Wait, this won't do at all. Annie, this won't do if you take that tone. You're all red. Have you gotten sunstroke?"

With an abrupt gesture, she freed her forearm, which he was still gripping hard. "You're hurting me."

"Could be. See these marks on my face? And I'm the one who's hurting you? You must be putting me on."

Now it was his turn to shake with anger, because not only was she close to attracting attention to them, she was also making him get the kind of splitting migraines only he got. He narrowed his eyes and added, "Kick up a fuss, Annie, and I swear to you you'll pay dearly for it, trust me."

"Then have a little respect for me."

"What? I have a lot of respect for you. Don't worry. If that's what's worrying you, I can reassure you of that."

She studied him wordlessly for a long moment. "You mean you don't get it? Is that possible? But you flirt with me, sweet-talk me to death, tell me to meet you, feel up my breasts, and then . . . nothing. You think that's normal?"

"Feel up your breasts? Now wait a minute . . ."

"When we were on that banquette."

"Oh, I see. You call that feeling up breasts? I grabbed the sugar dispenser, that's what happened. I grabbed the damn sugar dispenser because it was going to tip over, that's all."

He went inside to look for some Doliprane®. She followed. "Listen, Annie, be nice. Leave me alone for now. If you want, we'll see each other again tomorrow when class is over. I've got a very interesting proposition for you about those private lessons. A firm one. But you've got to understand, Annie. I can't promise to turn you into a writer. Nobody has that power. *That* we really have to agree on. I can teach you the whole caboodle and all the tricks of the trade; I can help you hold the pencil, scribble a few lines; but that's all I can do. I'm not a magician, okay? Take a recipe. Is using all the ingredients enough? Of course not. You need the gift. Your father can send me his goons again, and that won't change a thing. What we're talking about can't be converted into anything you can buy. If that were the case, I would have saved up a long time ago, Annie. I wouldn't be here teaching literature, I'd be writing it. You really need to understand that."

She looked hard at him again. "Listen. Let me tell you something. I actually don't understand a word you're saying to me. I just want to know why you're not attracted to me. I want to know what's wrong."

Outside of a few students who were a little drunk and were taking turns falling into one another's arms and not paying any attention to them, they were alone in the room. "Annie. Fine. If you're here to make my headache worse, say it. Say it right away. It'll save us some time. Why don't you help me find some aspirin instead? You know what would be nice? If we could shake hands."

"Go fuck yourself."

"Nice. At least you're being frank."

They opened several cupboards, some drawers. "Why did you do that to me?" she asked, handing him a package of aspirin she'd unearthed from a fruit bowl. He thanked her with a slight movement of his head.

"You should always have some of this on hand," he observed as he picked up a bottle of water. He swallowed the tablets. "Annie, think about it for a minute. Do you know what I'm risking if I get accused of having relations with a student? Take a good look at them," he said, pointing to the shady part of the yard where the teachers and their spouses stood. "What do you think of them? How much time would you give me before you saw my head roll? Obviously, I wouldn't be judged with as much disgust as an old pedophile priest, but almost, believe me. Look at 'em."

He lowered his eyes. "We better leave separately. Let things stay as they are for today. And talk about it all later, at a more appropriate time and place, don't you think? I'm really not myself today. You'd be amazing. I was so crude with you that I can hardly expect you to . . ."

"Kiss me. Take me in your arms and kiss me."

"Annie, Annie, Annie," he sighed. "I don't think you understood very well."

"Do it now. I'm giving you three seconds. Or the deal's off."

His hands closed quickly on Annie Eggbaum's shoulders—she was obviously no great beauty, but what a body; and he wanted to keep her from carrying out her threat, which could even amount to shouting sexual harassment if the idea came into her head. This was one determined student, not your common garden variety; and determination was one quality that was indispensable for a writer's career—but only one, and you needed a lot of others.

He forced himself to smile. "Kiss you how? On the mouth? Is that what you want?"

"And hold me in your arms while you're doing it."

"Annie," he said, shaking her gently, "wake up. It's not dark, and we're not on some remote country road. We're surrounded by people. Hello? It's a minefield out there for me. I might as well stick my head into a swarm of bees. Martinelli's there. The president, in person. Less than sixty feet away. Do you want to kill me?"

"Okay. Let's go into a bedroom."

"What? No, I'd rather stay here. We're going to do it here. It's in God's hands!"

"Think you can handle it?"

"I'll do my best."

He'd made up his mind to do it. Better to cut off a hand than an arm. Immediately she plunged her tongue into his mouth. He took advantage of it to grab her by the waist and spin around with her so they weren't in front of the window anymore.

There certainly were tougher chores, more repellent tasks. Annie was glued to him as if she were trying to make a mold of her body using his. She was also boldly caressing his neck and feeling his crotch. There was a time when he would have appreciated such passion, such an approach—someone had put on "Focus Please" by Be My Weapon, a song that was a must-have, and Annie's hair smelled nice—but the days when he'd had these feelings already seemed far away, as if they belonged to another time. Luckily, he'd been able to pull back all the way to the wall and was against it; a second more and he might have fallen backward with her on top of him.

He tried to muster up a maximum of spirit for the task, but his heart just wasn't in it. To put her off track, he put his hand on her ass and pressed his groin against hers. These gestures weren't too complicated to carry out, and he could see that they turned her on. His migraine hadn't gone away, but at least it hadn't gotten worse, so he pushed on resolutely. He bit her lips. That seemed to be a plus.

All in all, he came out of it well. He felt a bit badgered, but if this was the way to get out of this unfortunate situation, if this was the guarantee, he figured he was totally satisfied. There was no doubt about what a scare it had been, yet he'd handled it the best anybody could—reacting to the danger, pulling hard at the oars to keep from foundering. There'd be a reward. Regardless of everything, it had been a good lesson. Never drop your guard. He who did was dead. He'd had more than the usual amount of ordeals to testify to that.

A bottle rolled across the parquet. The din from outside barely reached them—asymmetric double glazing filled with argon. He saw a few blue plumes of smoke coming from the barbecue; the whole area reeked of it. The little group of students at the other end of the room seemed to have entered an advanced state of numbness, and that was also going to help matters. Meanwhile, the hands of the clock were turning, and Annie kept crossing swords inside his mouth with grim resolve, without showing the slightest sign of fatigue or any signal that this kiss would ever end.

When he wanted to push her away, she hung on to him even harder. "C'mon, be reasonable," he said, trying to loosen the stranglehold she had around his neck. "Stop acting like a child, would you. A promise is a promise. I was joking about a lot of things, Annie, but not about that. You asked for a kiss and got it. Isn't that what we just did?"

This little game could end up costing him a lot—somebody could come in at any moment. He pulled harder at Annie's arms, which stiffened around him even more. "Listen, it's simple enough. How can I trust you after this? Let's suppose we were to end up seeing each other. How could I, if you play tricks like this on me at the first opportunity?"

He yanked. She resisted. Obviously she had a lot of her father in her. He amped up his pressure. She grimaced. He twisted a wrist. Another young woman he'd known had refused point-blank to get out of bed, every time, to the extent that he'd had to pick her up, drag her to the edge of the mattress, and send her tumbling onto the floor, or she would refuse to get dressed. This was a little like that. The scenes women were capable of making. Unbelievable. *Too bad the outcomes were so often disastrous*, he thought to himself as he unfastened her from his neck, which she was hurting seriously at this point. Too bad they so often wound up in such a mess.

"Calm down," he repeated. "We'll talk about all this tomorrow, Annie. Anyhow, that kiss was dynamite."

"Dynamite?"

"Sure was. *Boom.* We're going to talk about all of it again. Promise. But not now. Tomorrow. Okay?"

She gazed up at him.

"Get going, now. You go out first," he said, pointing her in the right direction. "I said tomorrow, Annie. Now run along."

He watched her go off—after having given her one of his light slaps on the bottom, viewed, as a rule, in such a terrible light. Just as she was about to pass the big window, she turned around. "Dynamite," he uttered, giving her a thumbs-up. "Everything's cool, Annie."

It had been a close shave. Now that he saw her going back to the world, joining the others, the icy veil of fear—exactly that—slid along his shoulders for an instant, as he thought about what had just happened. The truth was that he'd almost gone to the edge. Really had. He'd come close to death, and that was the truth. He was exhausted. God knew what kind of a jam he'd be in now if he hadn't had adequate, instantaneous reflexes to the problems Annie caused. At this point, God knew into what kind of terrible vortex he was still endlessly falling these days, taking several others with him.

The thought of it brought back his migraine. He swallowed two or three more tablets and found a washbasin so he could cool his face and neck.

Making a narrow escape had a richness to it, but also a kind of violence, something close to orgasm that could be compared to parachute jumping—if what they said about it really was true. He splashed water on his face and neck for a while longer, then went back to the garden, pasting a casual expression on his face and without noticing the slightest lingering glance in his direction nor anything else out of the ordinary.

Marianne asked him where he'd been but barely listened to his answer; it didn't seem to interest her very much. It was early in the afternoon, and the sun beat down; most people were crowding into the shade where he was unlikely to find the peace he was hoping for and that he needed to pull himself together.

Richard Olso lived in a quiet, wooded neighborhood where every family must have owned a half-dozen vehicles, to judge by the near impossibility of parking nearby, without a miracle occurring. Slipping out discreetly was a cinch, as was straightening up in the street. But thinking about where he'd parked the Fiat became sheer torture, because of the terrible light falling from the sky—white, throbbing—more powerful than the five or six grams of aspirin he'd gulped.

Hesitantly, he covered the neighborhood the best he could, without seeing a soul who could tell him where he was.

He wandered around like that for at least a quarter of an hour, disoriented by the pressure on his temples—that gnawing, underground pounding of blood—as well as the flood of light pouring from the sky and making him squint because he'd left his sunglasses in the glove compartment.

The first thing he did was put them on the moment he climbed into his car. What a relief that was, to begin with. What a relief to be able to turn down the light, soften it some. He hung his head and for a long time kept his hands pressed against the steering wheel, his eyes closed; then he started the car and only just managed to drive away, swerving constantly to the left, verging on the other side of the road as cars coming the other way honked; or he'd go through a yellow light, which caused the same reactions that bore into his eardrums.

Until his nose began to bleed. At a red light, a woman studied him with glowering disgust mixed with fright, making him understand that something wasn't right. He glanced into the rearview mirror and saw the blood flowing down his chin, dribbling all the way to the front of his shirt. The other cars leaned on their horns because the light on the avenue had turned green and he wasn't moving. He was too busy frantically rummaging through his pockets in the hope of finding a handkerchief, or anything similar at all. Luckily, a roll of paper towels had been left on the backseat, so he tore off a few sheets and plastered them against his nose as a kind of collective hysteria took over the drivers behind him, who launched into a symphony of honks.

With one bloody hand awkwardly covering his nose, he put on his turn signal and cautiously cut across the right lane, but not without difficulty, since every one of his attempts at intrusion nearly caused an accident. But he needed to get out of the flow of traffic and take care of this umpteenth problem fate had laid on him and that required keeping his head tilted back, for lack of a better strategy.

He'd worked up quite a sweat. Nose bleeding, a raging migraine hounding him since morning; but at least he'd reached the emergency lane of the road. He turned off the motor, flipped on his hazard signal. It wasn't the best place to rest, but that was overshadowed by the relief he felt at having avoided a fatal accident on the beltway along the lake.

He kept his head tilted back, soaked up the blood with several more sheets of paper towel while the traffic rumbled next to him like an underground river. The blue sky of afternoon was changing in places to pink.

The police officer knocked on his window and gestured for him to open it.

He hesitated for a second, then made up his mind to do it, with fluttering eyelids. The police officer drew back at the sight of a face in such bad shape. "My God, what's happened to you, sir? Were you beat up?" Marc shook his head. "Are you in any shape to drive, sir?" He nodded. "In that case, sir, we'll begin by vacating the emergency lane. You'll take the first exit. I'll follow you." He was riding a motorcycle. Wearing a short-sleeved shirt. Looked as hard as nails.

When he was this overwrought, he usually went to his bedroom or found a dark corner as fast as he could, or made do with several covers over his head; it was better like that. The worst was to stay outside performing one of life's dismal daily obligations, such as putting up with the questioning of a police officer whose brain must have been the size of a marble, judging from that faint glimmer coming from his distrustful eyes.

"Sir, do you want me to take you to a hospital?" Marc shook

his head. "Are you sure?" Absolutely. So sure that each word pronounced by the policeman was like a sharp-edged stone somebody was trying to drive into his skull.

"Sir, are you under the effects of any drug?" He shook his head again. He was so annoyed, so full of contained rage. Was the steering wheel going to explode between his fingers? He remembered a chair rung he'd broken with his hands while his back was being thrashed with a belt. He'd always had powerful hands—as well as a pigheadedness that had to be taken in hand one way or another.

"Sir, take your hands off the wheel and get out of the car, please."

"Get out?"

"Sir, get out of this car. I'm not going to repeat it."

"No need to. I'm not deaf, you know. Let's not go overboard here."

He knew he was in no state to stand up to a police officer. His brain was about to explode, the blood beat against his temples, throbbed behind his eyes, coagulated in his nostrils. He'd known himself to be more resilient, but an impulse had seized him and he hadn't thought first, hadn't known how to rein in his first reflex. Sometimes, the cup overflowed, sometimes a person refused to be nothing more than a pitiful little puppet, and he got out wondering what the coming fit was going to cost him. He'd seen enough movies to have an idea of the methods keepers of the peace used.

The police officer had had them drive onto a service road, which had been overtaken by rubbish, thistles, rusted scrap iron, weeds.

"Sir, are you in possession of a weapon?"

119

"A weapon? Of course not."

"Sir, place your hands on the hood of the car. Spread your legs apart. I've got to make sure. I'm going to frisk you."

"Wait, I'm dreaming."

"Do as I say."

"Listen, I've got a headache worse than all tarnation."

"So do I."

*O*bviously, *the chances of finding her home at this hour* were slim. Night was falling, and the setting sun poured buttercup yellow from its low position. Its intensity would have required sunglasses, but those had ended up in pieces. What woman in Myriam's situation would have wanted to wander around her empty ghost of an apartment when the evening had hardly begun—unless she was planning on dying an inch at a time.

As for him, the question wasn't relevant. Not for a single second had he thought about staying alone in the state he was in; he was losing it and needed somebody at his side in case of an emergency.

Contrary to all expectation, a light was on in Myriam's window. He dragged himself to the intercom, gave his name, and slid to a sitting position against the door.

Later on, in the middle of the night, his eyes still open in the dark, he finally calmed down. She was asleep. His hands had stopped trembling, his panting had subsided, and his brain was no longer on the point of exploding. Even Marianne wasn't any better at taking care of him when he was like this, despite forty years of experience. He lit a cigarette. No light or sound came from outside. He turned toward her and drew nearer to take in her smell—her neck, shoulder, hip—moving his nose along her body a few millimeters from the surface of her skin. Reading someone that way often wasn't very easy, but in Myriam's case it was turning out to be really difficult. Several texts seemed entangled. Several images superimposed on one another. Not that there was anything unpleasant about it. Mysterious, obviously, but not at all unpleasant. On the contrary.

He wondered if he might have fainted between the moment he rang her doorbell and now. He couldn't remember a thing, Astounding. Day was immediately giving way to night.

Whatever had happened, he needed to be with this woman more every time. There wasn't much he could do about it.

Why hadn't he met her twenty or thirty years before, to gain time? What had been the use of all those young women, all those students? The shadow of Marianne flitted through his mind for an instant; then he put out his cigarette.

Sleeping with this woman seemed like his chance to stop being an adolescent. He couldn't have said whether they'd done it or not during the night, but his body felt like a recharged battery, and he wasn't going to regret it when the time came again to muster the energy to get through the woods.

So it had to come to this: that cursed police officer getting a heart attack, or whatever it was, practically in his arms. So something like that had had to happen. What a stroke of fate. If that wasn't cursed, then what did you call it? If that didn't beat all rotten luck, then what did?

Feeling sorry for himself wasn't going to help. Better to conserve his energy for efforts that would be worth the trouble. No choice but to accept the deal, as far as he was concerned. He had an unforeseen problem on his hands and was going to have to take care of it. You had to accept the cards you were dealt, if you didn't want to get thrown out of the game. He knew the rules.

He got up at the crack of dawn and dressed as he watched Myriam sleeping on her stomach, wearing only her brassiere. It was chilly outside; a thin sheet of translucent fog hovered over the lake, which was changing from gray to silver. He shivered, yawned, then got behind the wheel of the dew-covered Fiat, started it and backed into the road below, while keeping an eye on the flower beds the condo development was so proud of, and with good reason.

It was barely six in the morning, and the streets were deserted; ironically, he was taking the beltway again, the same road where the police officer had appeared a dozen hours ago. Then he was moving off toward the hills that were just emerging from darkness.

He checked out the area methodically before getting out. If things were a little out of hand, if the scene was tottering on its foundations, you had to be extra careful, become even tougher in order to keep your equilibrium. When he was certain there was nothing in the way, he put one foot outside and looked up at the path he was going to have to take with the body of the policeman on his shoulders. He sighed. The guy had to weigh around 175.

Merely getting him out of the backseat took several serious tries, not to mention the anguish he felt when he thought about being caught in the act, which laced the slightest move with hysteria.

By the time he'd hoisted him to his back and was ready to

start the climb, he was already sweating—and, for good measure, even covered with blood, completely smeared with it, whereas he was somebody who flinched at the slightest drop, the type who took the trouble to iron his trousers.

Certainly is hard not getting your hands dirty in this life, he thought to himself, as he moved through the undergrowth under his burden—these motorcycle cops weren't exactly little girls.

He was lucky to be in relatively good shape, when you took into account the number of cigarettes he'd gotten away with smoking nonstop. The rumor was that his mother hadn't stopped smoking for a single moment when she was pregnant, and that was why he and Marianne had the vice: it was buried in their genes. He pictured their father leaving the table without a word in the middle of the meal, because the smoke bothered him, as she waited for a reaction from him—as everybody waited for a reaction from him—and got nothing. Then you heard the door close, and the dishes began to fly.

In the early hours of morning, as the cock crowed, after a full three-quarters of an hour of uninterrupted effort, while the sun broke at the bottom of the valley, at the end of one of the most intense efforts of his life, he hauled himself up the final part of the path leading to the pit—that gaping mouth set back behind a damp, slippery protuberance. Good. Winded, pallid, shaking, he stopped for a moment. Then, under the first rays of the sun, listened to a cricket.

God knew the heap of problems he was avoiding in acting this way. The ordeal he'd just been through was nothing compared to the potential squabbles with the punctilious police, who were too often quick to see some miscarriage of justice. He blotted his forehead with an already damp handkerchief. It was going to be a beautiful morning. He was pleased about being able to settle this mess so quickly and smoothly, because he had a strong feeling that, very soon, other issues were bound to require the highest degree of attention. That police officer popping up out of nowhere. To begin with, it wasn't the kind of job you did if you had a weak heart. Unless you were a major nut.

He pushed the policeman's corpse to the far edge of the fault and then catapulted it in, using his two feet for leverage. Then he crept toward the pit to be sure that everything was in order, that nothing was visible, that the shadows were blotting it all out. Everything was perfect. This time, the officer's body had properly plunged straight down, avoiding the obstacle met by Barbara's.

At least this page had been turned. He let out a sigh, rolled onto his back. This pit was a veritable trump card. The sky was turning blue, crows flying, whirling, across it. Certainly the darkness of the pit released its share of negative energy that didn't make you want to come camping in the vicinity, but he thanked Heaven for having placed this terrible abyss in his path—even if he'd nearly been swallowed up by it himself. The pit was a true-blue ally. He'd hidden there for three days and three nights once, without moving, already getting ready to tremble in every limb when night would come, his teeth chattering in advance, moaning in anticipation like any child his age. . . . And yet, against all expectation, in complete contradiction to his morbid prognosis, he'd felt protected, secure, soothed; despite this cavernous silence and this endless blackness that had seemed to be hissing around him and had nothing to do with the thirst and hunger gnawing at him, despite the biting cold and the reprisals that were waiting for him in one way or another when they got their hands on him again, he'd considered himself relatively satisfied by his stay in its mineral and moss coziness. He seemed to be in solid with the creature that haunted this place. And it was capable of turning off the light and closing the door. Bolting the lock.

Closing his eyes, he almost fell asleep on the cold stone. The problem came from the fact that when he thought about Myriam now, his heart beat harder, his breath quickened. Difficult to ignore. Especially since this was such a new feeling, such an unknown one. Nobody had prepared him for it—the funniest thing was that he actually had written tons about such a feeling; no story would work without dealing with it or working it in in some way; and yet, irony came from the fact that he'd blackened thousands of pages describing something he knew nothing about. Mind-boggling, really. Quite a few of his characters had fallen in love, but what did he really know about it? Did he know what he was talking about? Today had brought the answers to these questions.

Regardless, the system he and Marianne had set in place and that had allowed them to get through four brave decades without too much fallout was about to be smashed to bits. He lifted himself onto his elbows and examined the tips of his shoes stained with blood.

Obviously, it would be better not to run into anyone in the filthy, blood-streaked shape he was in. He certainly could have claimed an inconveniently hemorrhaging nose as an excuse, though he looked more like a cranky horse butcher on his break than a decent man suffering from a nosebleed, no matter how severe.

Therefore it made sense to go down cautiously, keep an eye open to prevent any new incident from happening on the way back. He wasn't a big fan of that feeling of vulnerability experienced when you lose control of a situation, that feeling of gradually losing your cover, and he'd had more than his share of it these last few days. Not that he was against the unexpected, the kick of something new, a lesson, ups and downs, epiphanies; but didn't he need to get his strength back between each drill, instead of facing one after another or juggling them all at the same time?

He rubbed himself down with damp, dead, black leaves, in a kind of gross grooming session meant to allay suspicion in case of some unwanted encounter, or else to avoid being beaten up out there by a mental retard. It was still early enough. He certainly had more of a chance running into a doe in this area than any kind of nitwit, but he walked bent and silent, half running, taking advantage of the downward tilt of the ground.

He fell three times. The third time, his coccyx made a little noise and an icy flash went right through him. Even so, he got back up—surprised that luck wasn't in attendance these days and that this third fall had seemed bad enough to paralyze him, to keep him from reaching the car and leave him rotting in the woods with tears streaming down his face, howling with rage that nobody would hear. When he started walking again, he felt only a vague discomfort, and it faded away quickly.

As he got back behind the wheel of the Fiat, he let out a scream and jumped so high his head hit the ceiling. It felt like he'd sat on a tremendous needle.

He felt around down there with his hand, but there was nothing. No more pain, either; it had disappeared instantaneously—leaving behind some doubt about its authenticity. Firmly holding the steering wheel and gritting his teeth, he made a delicate attempt to sit down again, acutely anxious about the next setback fate might have in store for him.

Half reassured, and having finally settled in, he managed a few rotations of his pelvis, arched his back, bent forward, coughed, but without incident. Difficult to know what to trust, whether you were imagining things the entire day—a person and his body distrusted each other the majority of the time, though no one liked to talk about it and risk being unmasked.

"Why'd I ever think that we were ocean waves?" Frederick Seidel—the great Frederick Seidel—wonders in a recent poem. He looked at his watch. He'd asked his students to launch into several trains of thoughts starting at that line, and he had a little less than an hour before appearing in front of them in a change of clothes with his color restored, a clean body and a clear mind. He drove faster—took advantage of the fact that he was alone to do some completely tacky toe/heel pumps that his Fiat 500 would hardly appreciate after having racked up a total of 93,000 miles.

Marianne was still home—not very surprising. He went past the house and, after a minute, headed back the same way, shut off the motor. He entered from the back. In the entrance mirror he discovered how frightening he looked, and a weak groan escaped his lips at all the blood on his clothing, his face. He heard his sister in the kitchen, talking to the coffee machine. "Would you mind making it stronger for me this time? What—I didn't push the right button? Oh, come on now!"

He took advantage of this by slipping upstairs on tiptoe. If he did without breakfast, he could take a bath. After a second of hesitation, he turned on the bathtub faucets. When it came to cleanliness, he'd been well trained. Very well trained.

He got undressed. All his clothes were sticky, and they stunk. As the water gurgled out and misted up the bathroom, he checked himself out in the mirror. The blood had drawn rivulets on his face. No one would want to be seen in such a state, but that was how Marianne discovered him as he was about to step into the bathtub, with that gleaming mask covering his face and hands like a butcher's.

Everything he'd tried to avoid, obviously. Since she of course opened wide, horrified eyes and then slapped her hand over her mouth. Of course. What else could he have expected? And she didn't move an inch.

"Can't you see I'm not wearing a stitch?" he murmured.

There was no sense talking about it. Talking about it didn't help anything. She didn't like what she saw, and neither did he, to say the least, but there was nothing they could do about it. They weren't going to talk about it again. No. "We'll talk about it this evening; not now, please. Let me take my bath, okay? Don't make me late. You know they've got their eye on me. They're not going to let me get away with anything anymore."

He'd grabbed a towel and quickly wiped his face; all that steam, the mugginess of the place, contributed to a passable outcome, made his face seem almost acceptable, normal. Now, with the same towel, he hid his crotch.

When she'd had enough, she turned on her heels and quickly went back to her rooms on the ground floor.

By evening, he'd have found a way to present things to her that satisfied them both. He heard her car starting as he slid into the bathtub and lit a cigarette. As his coccyx touched the bottom of the tub, he winced again.

Certainly it was all scary. Such upheavals were scary. He got dressed in white and went out to teach class, already thinking about buying one of those small inflatable pillows shaped like a buoy, in anticipation of the suffering to come.

At noon, as he was putting away his stuff, thrilled at having unsettled half the class with the claim that literature isn't intended to describe reality—the other half were too greedy for fame to utter a sensible opinion about the issue. Annie began heading straight for him in her short skirt. If there was one thing about Annie Eggbaum, it was her persistence.

"Dynamite, Annie? I used the word *dynamite*? Frankly, that would surprise me. It's not in my vocabulary. Okay, then. It isn't important. Don't sit on my desk, Annie, be nice. You're obsessed, aren't you?"

"You kissed me."

"That's possible. Certainly is. People often do that. Look. Spring is here. People are making out from morning to night. In my day they called it messing around. I don't know what they say today. Really doesn't matter. We messed around a little. Of course. Is there a problem?"

He stared at her for a second while continuing to arrange the files inside his briefcase. Under normal circumstances, she would have been next, after Barbara; there was no doubt about it. She wasn't beautiful, but her cheekiness was a real turn-on.

"Just the opposite, everything's great," was her answer.

"Then good. You like the class?"

"I wouldn't know. I wasn't listening."

He smiled at her and started to walk out.

"I wasn't listening because I was fascinated by you, Marc. I was fascinated by you."

"Marc? You just called me by my first name?"

"Is there some other way I should call you?"

He sped up his walking. She followed. He stopped, touched her arm. "Listen, Annie. I'm going to speak frankly. This has nothing to do with you. Everything's fine concerning you. If that's what's torturing you, don't worry. No, it's your father. The problem's coming from him. You see, he makes me very uneasy. His methods make me very uneasy."

"Fine, I'll take care of that."

"Listen, Annie, I'd like to tell you I find that reassuring. I'm sorry, but I don't."

She seemed to be having trouble accepting someone not being attracted enough to her, and her lip was trembling. But would she be able to understand that another woman could capture his attention completely, dry up any other source of desire until further notice? Just as he was beginning to fear she'd make a scene, using the pretext that he wasn't making enough of an effort, as he was automatically checking things out over her shoulder, he caught sight of the detective at the other end of the hallway.

He quickly forced himself to look more relaxed.

"Let me get my calendar," he said, "and I'll tell you when I'm available. How's Wednesday? I'll figure out some way to get us a classroom. Okay?" For a fraction of a second his eyes had met those of the detective.

"You mean you agree to give me lessons?" she said, eyeing him suspiciously. "Is that really it?"

"Yes, seems so to me, wouldn't you say?" he answered,

pasting a big smile on his face. "Step away a little, would you? There."

If there had to be a real discussion between the two of them, a sound explanation, it wasn't going to take place here or now. Better to avoid making a spectacle in front of authority figures, giving an officer of the law a bad impression.

He scratched his head. "Does two hundred euros seem too expensive?"

"A month?"

"No, for the whole private class."

He got rid of her by mentioning Marianne, whom he supposedly had to get back to. Which he would, in fact, end up doing, figuring that meeting in the day would take some of the sting out of the confrontation that would take place that evening and was bound to be a trial. As he saw it, they wouldn't be in bed before dawn, and fairly in their cups by then.

Marianne's offices overlooked the campus. He greeted her with a friendly wave of the hand. Hey there. She froze. Apparently, then, there'd hardly been any progress since morning, except that she wasn't covering her mouth anymore. He gestured for her to pick up her cell phone. He turned his on. "Want to go out and have coffee with me? I'd enjoy it."

She opened her mouth, but he heard only her breathing, incredibly near, amplified as it was by the device.

"Everything's okay," he went on. "Everything's fine. Pull yourself together. Then how about an ice cream. Want me to take you for ice cream in this beautiful weather? Wadda ya say? Would you stop staring at me with that long face? I'd appreciate it, you know. Don't forget I'm your brother."

"No. No ice cream. Thanks."

"You're right. It's fattening. We can go lie in the grass. Calm down. Everything's fine."

"Everything's fine? You dare say that to me? Go fuck your-self."

She hung up. Without moving her eyes off him, she folded her cell phone closed and stuck it in her pocket. Normally, she didn't use such coarse language. It was an excellent gauge of her mood. She called back. "Go fuck yourself," she repeated, and hung up. Such repetition indicated a level that was close to white-hot. Obviously, she was referring to vows he'd made, promises, etc., but could she honestly blame him for not having kept them; could she ever doubt his sincerity?

She turned the slats of the shutters to shut out the sight of him, but he'd already left and was heading for the parking lot, figuring that their talk had been fruitful. First words had been exchanged. What they said wasn't so important. That was minor.

He found Myriam at home in the middle of the afternoon. They got undressed and, later, as they were smoking a cigarette, he told her something about what he and Marianne had been through; he opened up a little. She listened, caressing his face. The afternoon was ending. "And that's made my sister and me very close."

"I can imagine. I really can understand."

"Well, yes, but sometimes it can get to feel like a burden, I admit. But I haven't forgotten that she's the one who saved my life. Didn't I tell you about that? It so happens that one day I fell into a crevice, somewhere in this forest. I wouldn't be here to tell you about it if Marianne hadn't grabbed my hand and helped me get back up. That shows how close we are."

With time, he'd become expert at making smoke rings. He could send them to the ceiling when he wanted to or make them float in place like scraggly, quivering donuts with currents of air circling through them. For a brief moment, his mind wandered as he devoted himself to this. He thought ahead to the discussion he was going to have with his sister. He had a holy terror of talking about such things, bringing them up, trying to pull them out of the dense darkness around them; but he honestly knew almost nothing about such things. Still, he knew he couldn't avoid them.

Looking at Myriam, he finally came to the conclusion that he'd always had an inordinate penchant for milky-skinned redheads. He put out his cigarette and lowered his eyes. His sister wasn't about to stop clapping a hand over her mouth—maybe biting her fingers even—if he kept overwhelming her, furnishing her with deeply bitter and resentful subjects, like the ones he'd been piling on recently. So there was little chance of her receiving the news of his new, more and more profound relationship with Myriam in an even-tempered and benevolent way.

Would it drive her closer to Richard Olso, the man he hated more than anybody in the world, the man who got infatuated surprisingly regularly with lousy books and lousy authors, contributing to the spread of literature that was dull, depthless, uninspired, and never surprising?

*T*he first session he gave Annie Eggbaum—at a high price, after she insisted that he come to her place—took place at the edge of her swimming pool in late afternoon, with the sun sparkling silently on the faraway summits of the Alps and the weather still very mild. Summer seemed to have come in a flash.

Annie was wearing a bathing suit. A simple bikini. She'd prepared some cocktails with fruit. Served in large glasses. Embellished with thick novelty straws. She had placed three hundred euros on the table.

"It's really three hundred euros? For one hour? In cash?" she'd asked with an ingenuous expression. He'd nodded and taken the money, calmly slipped it into his wallet. The cheapest bodyguard cost ten times as much; the most minor soccer player earned enough to buy half this city; the lowest-paid banker had enough economic muscle to throw entire families into the street. Three hundred euros didn't mean much in comparison to certain sums put into certain hands in every city, country, continent. Three hundred euros were about as important as one tear in the eye of a crocodile on one Lacoste shirt, a microscopic speck of dust at the outermost corners of the world.

"Why did you sign up for my course, Annie?" She didn't answer. He himself didn't attach much importance to the explanations she'd be able to furnish. He was holding his glass in one hand and his cigarette in the other, staring at the swimming pool and thinking what ideal weather it was for a dip.

"Go for it. Indulge yourself. I'll find you a bathing suit."

The trap was so transparent that he snickered. Had he expected anything else, deep down? This girl was completely out of her mind. So out of her mind, in fact, that you avoided putting her on the defensive without good reason. However, he turned down the offer to go swimming and suggested they take another look at the work she'd recently handed in. It was pretty bad.

"See that window?" She was pointing to a French window on the third floor, opening onto a flowered balcony. "That's my room."

He let out a quiet sigh. Too many other thoughts were going through his mind as she extended a hand to him, her chest thrust forward. It wasn't Annie Eggbaum he wanted to be with at that moment.

He ignored her invitation. "Tell me, Annie," he said, pulling some pages from his briefcase, "didn't anybody ever tell you the semicolon was dead?"

Without giving her time to react, he placed his hand on his heart and asked her to do the same. "Feel that? Does it tell you anything? Listen, Annie, I think we're going to have to talk about rhythm. I think you're going to have to open your ears."

He was trying to keep his distance. And yet, when you were dealing with a truly determined woman, you rarely won any early hands. So he'd chosen not to sit down and stayed on the other side of the table when he had to come nearer to see what she'd written and the corrections he'd made in the margins.

Unlike his friend Barbara, she wasn't gifted, so he was able to keep her in check during the first half hour while confronting her with her weaknesses, with the efforts she'd need to give a sentence good rhythm, good impetus, etc., without seeming like a body builder doing a workout, if at all possible.

The day was ending. No sound came from the house. It was a large one in the modern style, with big picture windows. Suddenly, he heard a splash. He looked up as he was reminding his student of the suppleness and severity of a snake, to give her a little more precise idea of the minimum expected of anybody who expected to get published, how that person should, at least, keep the image of a snake in mind—its fluidity and hardness.

She reappeared. "Come on in!" she called out to him, dripping wet.

He preferred taking his place on a chaise longue.

"We're the only ones at the house," she explained, shooting up level with his chaise longue, like a mermaid.

He'd almost figured so. Not long ago, he would have easily given in to this girl's desires. The matter would have been settled. But things had changed. Mountains had crumbled, peaks had settled into valleys.

"You think you can use reason to deal with this kind of thing?" she reprimanded in a flat voice. "You think I don't know everything you'd like to say to me? All this bullshit."

"What bullshit? I haven't said a word. Stop with the groundless accusations, if you don't mind. Annie: everybody knows that this kind of thing can happen. It'll pass. Look at me. I'm fifty-three. You deserve better than that. I knew a girl your age who thought she was in love with Jankélévitch. She didn't miss a single class but didn't listen to a friggin' word he said."

She slapped the surface of the water, splashing it in his direction without reaching him. He lit a cigarette, imagining the sadness of a life without tobacco. Below them the lights of the city shone, but around them it was silent, barely disturbed by the chirping of insects and the cries of birds flying across the sky at dusk.

He took a few puffs. "Has it ever occurred to you I might have someone?" he asked. "It never entered your mind?"

"I'm not jealous. Are you talking about that woman?"

"I don't know. Who, for example?"

"Not too young."

"Exactly."

She found him some Ralph Lauren swimming trunks, on hand for unprepared visitors, and he congratulated himself for having yielded, because the beginnings of another migraine disappeared almost immediately—water treated with active oxygen obviously wasn't in the reach of every pocket, but oh how pleasant it was, oh how enthusiastically you'd like to recommend such a system, oh how soft it made your skin.

"She's closer to my generation. You see what I mean. I can develop certain feelings for her that I can't have for you, Annie. You ought to understand. After a certain time, the mental plays a much more important role. Maybe I'm at a turning point in my life, you know. I know that doesn't make it very cool for you, I'm perfectly aware of it, but imagine yourself at a crossroads, put yourself in my place for a second." Both of them were resting on their elbows at the edge of the pool; their bodies floated underwater, just below the surface. Hair damp and expressions unchanging, they studied each other for a moment among the soft lapping of water and the hooting coming from the woods. Then she drew her leg back like a spring and pretended to push him away or kick him as punishment, but she did it very gently, with hardly any force. Pulling a long, sullen face. She tried the kick again. Without really reaching him. It looked like she wanted to have a kind of wrestling bout with him, or at least some rough horseplay.

The fact that she was disappointed went without saying. It was written all over her face. But she showed she was more reasonable than he had expected, and in the end kept quiet, stopped raising her fist at him.

There were soft, white, carefully folded beach robes waiting for them. As soon as he'd put one on, he hurried to his cigarettes—the first puff taken at dusk can be a superb high for the somewhat serious aficionado. He picked up his cocktail with one hand and made a friendly gesture toward Annie, who was floating near the edge. It was all becoming very pleasant, relaxing. The air was beginning to smell of ripe wood and lake; the sky was growing darker. Suddenly Annie was revealed in a much less terrible light. If she wanted to and was willing to put a minimum of work into it, he could guide her to produce work that was average for the times—to the point of being able to sign good contracts with publishers, and maybe even cop a few foreign translations. The rules weren't that hard to follow— weren't there some very bad writers nimbler than monkeys who managed to climb to the top of the ladder? She wouldn't end up one of the worst if he gave her some good writers to read, made her fill page after page, and taught her the art of provocation.

"Afghanistan is going to become a new Vietnam, everybody knows it. Anyway, she hasn't heard from him in months. Yep. Personally, I think he's not about to come back. I'm pretty sure we're losing more men than they want to tell us. Freezing at night, scorching during the day. That damn country's one big trap. I'd be surprised if he came back at all, to be honest."

She pulled a face, then did a few lengths in the evening air.

Next he helped her out of the pool by extending a hand to hoist her up, acting thrilled with his catch and moving in a way that triggered such a violent pain near his last vertebra that he was in shock for a split second. He froze, like an animal at bay in the light of the moon. Tears rose to his eyes. Blinking them away, he crashed onto the nearest mattress somewhat terrified, as if struck by an acute bout of tetany.

He managed enough breath to explain that his coccyx had turned to crumbs and that he figured he'd rest for a few minutes before deciding what to try next, even if it only amounted to blinking. "Unfortunately, nothing can be done, unless you have something very strong," he sighed, his heart still pounding in his chest. She came back right away with some pink pills that he gulped down unhesitatingly, because death itself was nothing compared to the unbearable flash of pain that had struck him a moment ago.

He thought of the distance to his car and the fact that he'd never be able to make it without crutches if the agony continued. The situation reminded him of some very bad moments—including the time he fell on the kitchen tiles, after she'd knocked over his chair by kicking him in the chest, because he was defending his sister: horrible memory of a time when insanity at home was raging and maximum brutality was the rule, when staying on the ground was often the best available solution.

The swimming pool lit up automatically. The small of his back was so tensed from fear of having to suffer another bout of this sort of electric discharge that he couldn't relax it any longer. A knot had formed, a block of pain that tolerated only total immobility—no creams, massage, nothing else would work; and all he wanted to do was keep lying there for a moment, to get his breath back, not move.

His joints felt so stiff and his nerves were so on edge that he barely managed to sit up when Christian Eggbaum, her father—the same man who'd so generously treated him to that thrashing by way of his henchmen—arrived. Marc excused himself, awkwardly straightened the beach robe over his thighs, and explained that he'd suddenly been stricken with muscle paralysis in the lumbar region. "I know who you are," answered his host. "You're my daughter's teacher." As he said it, he came toward him with a gracious smile and extended a hand.

Later, both father and daughter helped him to the Fiat, although he refused to let them take him home with the pretext that he'd never let anyone do it, never on that road, etc. They propped him up from either side, encouraging each step as if he were a family member for whom they were responsible. The man didn't look like a vulgar mafioso, or bank robber hardened by nightclub scuffles; he looked a lot more like one of today's financial confidence men who care about the cut of their shirt and their choice of cologne, which in this case happened to be Five O'Clock Au Gingembre, by Serge Lutens.

Strange people. Annie's tablets began working during the drive back, now that those two kind souls had gently placed

141

him on the buoy-shaped cushion he'd bought a few days ago and he was alone at the wheel of his car, as he left the city and drove up the hill toward his place and stars appeared in the black sky over the forest.

He was in no condition to drive. He had to have the sense of the road at his fingertips to keep from flipping over into a ditch or smashing into the barrier and hurtling in a horrendous somersault to the bottom of the mountain. The road snaked, but he kept the correct path in his head and adjusted to some degree, managing to keep to his lane without too many mishaps. As long as nobody was coming the other way.

Nevertheless, seated with the small of his back nicely propped up and coccyx free of contact (thanks to that hideous donut pillow—they really were something of a miracle), seemed to make things okay. He straightened slightly—something he wasn't able to do a few moments before when the Eggbaums put him into his car and asked him to promise to come back as soon as he was back on his feet.

Once home, however, he honked his horn: no need to be foolhardy and get struck down because of overconfidence when he was so near his destination. He needed Marianne to help pry him out of the tin can he'd been driving that seemed to have been designed for midgets. He honked again, but nobody came. Then he leaned forward slightly and discovered Richard Olso's Alfa parked on the shoulder.

He lowered his window and heard more or less human-sounding cries of rage coming from the house. Like a herd having their throats cut. Or was it dogs barking? Sirens. Helicopters. Shooting. A deafening chorus. Even so, the area around the house looked a picture of calm. A wispy plume of white smoke escaped from the chimney and vanished into the starry firmament, which was untroubled by the slightest cloud. Mountaintops twinkled in the moonlight, and the lake's placid waters sparkled through the woods as deer went by, squirrels nibbled nuts, and birds of prey glided through the mild air.

Slipping a cigarette between his lips, he grit his teeth, opened the car door. Dragged himself from his seat, relying completely on the strength of his arms. Once he was standing in the soft calm of the evening, as the racket from the house reached a peak, he checked that his balance was good enough for flicking his lighter and lit up a smoke, before starting to walk. Today, every cigarette seemed incredibly delicious.

The walls of the house were shaking. An especially violent scene from *Apocalypse Now* was playing, and Richard Olso was at the controls. It was unbelievable, but true. That unbearable din shaking the entire house was nothing less than the handiwork of that appalling cretin Richard, who'd turned into a sound engineer.

"This is incredible," Marianne announced. "It feels like you're there."

Apparently, the poor girl had finally snapped. "What the hell are you talking about?" he fired at her, without so much as a glance at Richard Olso. "But first of all, what is this stuff?"

"Marc, old man, it's about turning the living room into a movie theater. I'm going to give you a demonstration. Sit down."

"Marianne, I've smashed my coccyx to smithereens. It took me fifteen minutes to get across the yard. Inch by inch. Oh, and yes, thanks for the help. It was priceless. Without you I don't know how I would have made it here."

"Wait, Marc, you're putting us on."

"Stay out of this. Don't try to come between me and my sister. You're wasting your time."

All of a sudden, Marianne stood up from the couch and aimed at the screen, which went black on the image of Dennis Hopper's lunatic scowl. "First of all, where were you?" she came out with, skimming past him.

"Where? I told you. Giving lessons."

He was looking at her back and bare shoulders as she stood in front of the picture window, which the darkness had turned into a mirror. He made a gesture indicating he actually didn't give a good goddamn about any of it and headed toward the stairs to his room, refusing to put up with those two any longer; a few minutes were too much.

Grabbing hold of the banister with both hands, he grit his teeth and launched into the first steps. Would he be in any shape to face class in less than twelve hours? He'd always been aware of having to set an example as a teacher, and steady attendance was part of what he needed to impart to novice writers: sitting down at your desk whether you wanted to or not, writing daily and relentlessly, revising phrases and words, day after day, relentlessly, never acting like an amateur, or shirking. During all these years, he'd been absent barely more than two or three times; and on some occasions, he'd been little short of heroic, because he'd felt so indisposed, and it was so difficult. Nor did he want to add to the list of the hundreds of millions of unemployed these days wandering the world half-naked, their entire families foundering, despite the faultless assistance of the banks.

He made it upstairs, his forehead damp with sweat. Exacerbated by Richard's presence, as much as by Marianne's attitude. This was the second time this week he'd found Richard Olso in their house; he couldn't accept such frequency. How long before he'd be seeing him at their table? How long before he'd run into him early in the morning, wearing a bathrobe? Yodeling in the shower? What grotesque game was Marianne suddenly playing? What was the point of it?

He swallowed a few pills, got undressed, brushed his teeth, as the Alfa went into motion beneath his windows. By the time he made it to bed, its motor was already a distant wail. He lowered the lights, lay down. Almost immediately, the image of Myriam popped into his mind, and his breath quickened slightly. Truly disconcerting: these feelings were more intense than everything he'd ever experienced before, everything he'd ever even imagined. Not being able to hold her in his arms was beginning to hurt—not being able to smell her, penetrate her, talk to her.

He lit a last cigarette and sighed with ease at the feeling of the pills kicking in, at the definite arrival of their euphoric effect. He closed his eyes.

When he opened them again, Marianne was sitting on his bed. "I didn't know you were still interested in me," she confessed. "I'm happy about it."

He propped himself up on his elbows. The navy-blue briefs he was wearing had absolutely nothing indecent about them, and this was his room; but he felt as if he were being accused of something in some way or other. She lit a cigarette and sent a few puffs in the direction of the moonlight that was washing the forest with a silvery sheen. They floated upward, veneering the ceiling.

"But what am I supposed to do?" she murmured after a moment. "Tell me what I'm supposed to do? Wait for you to announce the news? Wait for the day you move out? Wait until I end up alone?"

He could tell she'd been drinking. He caught hold of her wrist and brought the cigarette she was holding to his lips as she watched him do it. "How long have you been thinking about this ending-up-alone business?" he said, blowing smoke. "Since when has Richard Olso become a viable option for any situation at all? Since when has a guy who confuses having talent with acting smart been able to interest you for any length of time? Did he drug you? Then what? Acting smart is great for drawing up lists, but . . ."

Obviously, it was ungrateful of him to reproach Marianne for having used her powers of attraction in one way or another to get him out of some tight spots. He was totally aware of it. If she hadn't stepped in, he'd have lost his job. It was true; without those few opportunely timed tête-à-têtes with Richard to plead his case, he'd have been let go without further consideration. Et cetera. He knew it. But this was stronger than he was; some kind of drill was spiraling through his guts.

He felt as if they were losing something, but he hadn't found any way to stop the bleeding. God knew that they stuck together, had developed a special relationship during the time when their mother had such contempt for it and would sneer about "those two virgins being *glued* to each other." God knew how much they meant to each other—if not, where would he have found the strength to accomplish what he had; if not, what kind of uncontrollable rage would have worked its way to the surface?

But now? Where were they now? All he could do was hold her tightly against his body, and that was how they stayed, wordlessly. Then she started weeping silently, shed some tears. She turned around to face him again, enlacing her legs with his. He understood perfectly what she was feeling, her fear of abandonment, stemming from those grim years. Only he could stave it off by holding her in his arms, his legs, as if he were building a strong barrier around her for as long as necessary; and it worked even better when they used a blanket that he'd throw over his shoulders, draping it around him like the canvas of a poorly staked tent.

The skirt bothered her, so she slipped out of it; but, like him, she left on her underwear. Most of the time, they stopped when they got to that point and stayed entwined that way, sleeping as naturally as could be, and feeling reassured, soothed. But there were times when they'd gone all the way without even being completely aware of it; it flowed from their embrace, or a kind of giving up, or from the fact that they were shaking, or rubbing together for a long time, or from alcohol and other substances, from grief; and suddenly, it would be too late, he would be inside her without having at all thought about it in advance, without even having put his hands there; and then no one said another word—or would say anything in the morning or evening or the days that followed. Neither felt any need to and thanked the other silently for not broaching the subject.

Obviously, once they'd gone too far they'd enjoyed it; but there was nothing very "sexual" about it, in the current sense of the term. It had more to do with an optimum mental connection, a raging need to lock down together as tightly as possible against the violence of the winds. And there was a pleasure they found in it, almost as if it were a religious experience, something that purely and simply produced transcendence. On the night of the fire, when they crouched in a broom closet in the cellar, hadn't he stifled a sob just as he spilled into her?

The last time they had relations had been that winter, after the Christmas Eve that both had been toasting a little too enthusiastically—forced as he'd been again to confront his perpetual bitterness about neither of them having any friends and living kind of like savages at the edge of the road, but still in the middle of the woods, the closest neighbor being more than a third of a mile out of view and lost in an ocean of vegetation. In fact, they were no more than marginal members of their community, even if they were saved by the luck of being white and having no accent.

He'd been justified for what had happened, but never completely forgiven. When it came to Marianne, other women acted reserved, disapproved in no uncertain terms of the strange dyad made up of the two of them, or they simply saw it as unhealthy. The oldest women were the most understanding, moved as they were by their history of child abuse, which had made the local papers.

Sometimes, having a few drinks seemed to be their last and only resort, or, at the very least, a friendly strip of land you had to head for as quickly as possible to avoid a horrible Christmas Eve for two, marked by zero-percent-fat cottage cheese.

A fine layer of snow had fallen the day before that day, and the area had had a pleasant powdery look. It wasn't late yet. Sunset was plunging into a luminous cauldron that throbbed silently, surrounded by flames as Father Christmas got ready to descend to Earth.

He hadn't changed his clothes yet. What was the hurry? He wondered if he'd go and shave or watch a film to pass the time and wend his way slowly toward evening.

Facing the picture window, she commented on how fascinating the light was and asked for her first drink. It was just after four in the afternoon, but she insisted, pressuring him to get her one so that she could keep her eyes on that magnificent, amazingly soothing snow-covered landscape, give it all the attention it deserved. He opened his mouth to speak but remained silent. He was already planning on hooking up again with that new student he hadn't been seeing for very long, if he could put Marianne to bed before it got too late.

Admittedly, joining that young woman was the most pressing thing on his mind. This happened every time one of these girls entered his life. What a relief it was. What a breath of fresh air—at first, anyway. So he complied, fixed two gin martinis, hoping she wouldn't stick to that rhythm for too long a time and that he'd be able to give her the slip after putting her to bed with a damp towel on her forehead. They clinked glasses as a family of rabbits were crossing the road single file, backlit against the absolute whiteness. "Be nice and pour me another," she said, after the last rabbit in line had disappeared into the undergrowth.

Neither of them could claim having been exempt from fate, but he refused to follow his sister into one of those jags of depression she had at regular intervals. He'd protest that they also had very good reasons to thank heaven for being alive and for having been granted a relatively normal—privileged, in fact— life, after such disastrous beginnings.

She hadn't made it to winter in very good shape. Her state

of mind had kept deteriorating until the holidays, which she was preparing to go through like a zombie. Sometimes, he'd find her sitting in a corner, even on the ground with her knees folded, all bones in her silky pajamas that were usually too big for her. He'd take her in his arms to help her back to her room.

Good sport that he was, he cautioned her about the drawbacks of pulling such an early drunk in the middle of the afternoon, although twilight was already glazing the mountaintops gold. It made no sense when a party was looming on the horizon and they were bravely hoping to hold on as long as possible to keep from seeming too pathetic. The rabbits were barely out of sight before she began shrugging at his advice and poured herself another. Then her bathrobe fell open, and the soft funnel of a lovely bare breast tipped by her nipple made its appearance; she took her time putting it back because her reaction time was already dulled.

He avoided her eyes. Put a log into the fireplace, which released sparks. She lay down on the couch facing the hearth, which was soon the only source of light. In the late days of December, night fell with astounding rapidity. He decided to sit on the carpet with his back pressed against the couch. "I'm looking forward to eating lobster," he said, realizing that the sentence might seem puzzling. She chuckled. She must have discovered his affair with the student, it occurred to him, and was staggering under the blow, even though he'd always been careful to do what he did out of sight, especially when it came to Marianne. Her bitter, reproachful silences tinged with confused helplessness and anger had nothing to do with chance.

Sometimes, no matter how much they bit their fists to keep

from crying out, certain noises unfortunately escaped from the girls' throats that could easily be heard all the way downstairs, without any major effort at listening. He was the first to regret it. He'd always preferred the thrashings they gave him to the simple slaps Marianne got. Their mother had understood this quickly enough: she began grabbing the poor girl by the hair and shaking her until she agreed to come out of her hiding place for punishment reserved exclusively for her.

He figured she'd had her share of suffering. He didn't want to add to it. Letting his neck fall backward, he pressed his head against his sister's thigh as a way of establishing contact; any sign of affection, commitment, warmth, no matter how tenuous, was welcome in such situations. He had to be especially considerate with her. He lit a cigarette and gave it to her. How could he be the way he was? What kind of unspeakable heart did it mean was beating in his chest? How could he be the one to make her worry, live in fear?

He could feel the heat of the hissing flames that were in front of him on his forehead and cheeks, as the icy air outside sent flakes down from the heights to cover the Christmas lights, clocks, and illuminated decorations they'd installed in the streets without much imagination—and certainly without much of a budget, because of the wide-ranging restrictions still in force. He felt Marianne's hand in his hair. As a child he'd loved having his hair styled, his scalp touched, and he willingly surrendered to his sister's hands. Merely a comb passed through his hair could make him quiver to the tips of his toes; parting his hair gave him goosebumps; and getting shampooed, well, that was a guaranteed erection. Remembering such moments brought a smile to his lips—unless it was because of the antidepressants.

151

Their father used Palmolive Brilliantine. A truly flowing, perfumed effect.

Today, six months later, he barely remembered that Christmas Eve. Nothing about it had stayed in his mind, except that it was the last time they'd had sexual relations together. He didn't know how they'd ended up giving in—*giving in* was the term— but the tiled floor of the bathroom was hard and cold, and the thin bath mat he'd managed to slip under their backsides hadn't turned out to be much help.

Today, in the balminess of June, they were about to begin again. They were lying on the bed in their underpants, in the darkness, and they rolled from one edge to the other, enlaced in that disquieting darkness, their exhilaration building, as if someone had tied them together. The fact that he was capable of this type of behavior in the utterly handicapped state he'd been in a few minutes earlier had something of the miracle about it.

During their tight embrace, he thought about how distant he'd acted with her lately, and this upset him. How could he have done such a thing, he kept repeating to himself, how could he have failed in his role to such an extent. At any rate, despite her scrawniness, Marianne had an ample chest. He buried his face in it before beginning to suck the violet-pink tips, which were shaped like limpets.

He needed to be very kind to her. Make up for the lack of attention he'd shown her. But at the same time, he couldn't help thinking of her relationship with Richard, and he had to hold in an urge to strangle her. Maybe he didn't know the details, but that didn't mean that the two being together wasn't intensely unpleasant for him. Imagining Richard Olso possessing Marianne, kneading her breasts, slobbering over her like a goat, panting, and coming on her face, etc., knocked the wind out of him.

Then they fell headlong into it.

In the morning, as he was drinking his coffee, he went to the living room and came across the hi-fi equipment that Richard had been blasting the day before. Since when had that idiot been fooling around with this kind of stuff? He dropped onto the couch on which he'd found them the day before, practically sprawled on top of each other. Then he looked up. He saw a fifty-inch flat-screen with surround-sound speakers on high stands. He picked up the remote and chanced upon a mudslide that had swept away a village in the Far East. Cows, roosters, dogs, people had all ended up in the same boat. The screen image was high-resolution, accurate, and radiant. The sky was a silvered dark gray, and you could make out all the details. In a few days, as much water had fallen as during the entire year, and the disturbing, swirling depth of the sky was a sign of those furious winds on the other side of the world at times when one electrified current rumbled within another, trying to be the one to pull the blackest curtain, the densest fog that would smother sounds and bog down minds to the greatest extent possible.

Even though he was no expert in feminine sexual matters, the harshness and severity with which Marianne conducted their relationship somewhat disturbed him. Most of the time, she ended up on top of him, subjecting her womb to some kind of joyride and half-sobbing. It wasn't very healthy, and he knew it. But it wasn't his place to judge what was healthy when it came to such things. He went out to the garden to get some air. The sun was rising, and he could smell the green leaves. A luminous mist hovered over the lake. Through the material of his pajamas, which he was wearing without the top, he gently palpated his coccyx. Things seemed to have gotten better in that respect. He'd only slept a few hours, but it had been a deep sleep, because she'd come back to his room a moment later, like a thief, after a pit stop at the bathroom upstairs; he expected her to break a bone someday by tumbling down the steps leading to his quarters.

He lit a cigarette as a faraway dog barked, and a cuckoo sang loudly in a nearby tree. The police officer's disappearance remained a mystery. His colleagues had no doubts at this point about his being dead, and tests confirmed that a sample of blood taken from an entrance ramp to the highway was definitely his. The fact that there was a cop killer in the city—like some kind of armed loony set loose in the wild, or rather, in a neighborhood high school or supermarket—was no laughing matter for anybody and didn't help the image of the police, who immediately started being viewed as good-for-nothings and dunces. He had to be doubly cautious, remain on alert. The police were investigating with a vengeance, and there was still a danger that they'd trace the car to a certain teacher who was living with his sister in the hills.

He'd rechecked the pit a few days ago; at night, in fact, because it offered the most protection. He lit his way with a good flashlight and was equipped with sturdy shoes and a rope. This was before he'd helped Annie Eggbaum out of her swimming pool and added a sprained back to his fractured coccyx, so getting down there, once he'd carefully attached himself to the rope for safety purposes, had gone off smoothly, without even disturbing an owl hooting above him as he took hold of the roots and bushes growing along the wall.

There was no stink coming from the place. No corpse visible. Lying on the outer edge of the rock spur that had first gotten in the way of Barbara's corpse, he'd methodically scoured the depths with his flashlight and finished his inspection with a satisfied look. This pit wasn't going to betray him any time soon. It was nowhere near the time for any body or carcass to be pulled from it; it looked as if it went downward endlessly.

Before climbing back up, he sat on his heels and smoked a cigarette, the light revealing several bats in some places, some mosses in others; and he heard some vague sounds of runoff as a starry disc of sky hovered above his head. He loved being in this place. Now he had more proof of it. Every time he climbed down, he felt strangely protected; every time he found himself surrounded by that wall of rock, he could breathe, succeed in relaxing entirely, clear everything from his mind. It was lucky, wonderfully lucky, that the nicotine usually put him in a dazed state, and he prayed to heaven that such an outstanding effect would recur until the end of time, that there'd never be an end to such happiness. It wasn't just smoking that could kill you in this life—there was a whole range of things.

When his sister opened her window, pulling him from his thoughts, a radiant, though sulky, version of her appeared to him. That was how their encounters usually wound up: an evasive wryness took over her face that he really didn't know how to interpret, but the darkness faded in a day or two and was often extended by quite a long stretch of tranquility, good morale, less tension.

He gestured to her. Would have liked to know more about the new equipment in the living room, but he was going to have to wait.

He took advantage of the wait by mowing the lawn and went back as often as possible to Myriam's two-room apartment in the city, whose door chimes made him tremble all the way to the tips of his toes. Right now, as often as possible meant around twice a day: in the morning, before his writing workshop, and at the end of the afternoon, or at least before nightfall, before going home. Often enough to ensure he'd teach excellent classes that were practical, crisp, popular, appreciated more and more by the students (Annie Eggbaum hadn't been the last to want to express her admiration and enthusiasm), although no one knew that the sex he was having with such zeal and regularity was largely responsible for it.

Most of the writers in this country weren't worth a dime. They were the perfect examples of bad writing. Excellent examples. His students would laugh. He hoped that if he couldn't make good writers out of them, he'd at least make them into good readers. Readers who knew how to listen. He'd line them up and begin reading a page of Raymond Carver, or someone else on that level, marking the cadence with his foot and fingers, and when they felt ready, when they had understood what was happening, each would add his or her voice to his, according to the rhythm. Then new readers joined in, and it became a roaring torrent. In fact, the young people did understand. You had to spend quite a long time explaining things, sometimes insist on them, but they caught the cadence a lot more quickly than the old bastards who put you to sleep by steering a middle course. And that was why he didn't regret not being a writer, not having anything to do with these people; when it came to them, he preferred not having gotten his hands wet.

Myriam agreed. Not that she held herself up as any

authority on the matter, but he'd already lectured her at length about poverty and glory of style, the detailed choices that come into play at every moment; the different conflicts that can proliferate within the same phrase; the sacrifices that had to be granted; the absolute priority of language, dynamism, resilience, fine-tuning, necessity, giving in. She began to have a few serious notions about the subject. It obviously wasn't her favorite food for conversation; she much preferred hearing the story of all the horrors he'd experienced, and what miracle had brought him out of them, right up to the final act. But she listened to him without showing the slightest sign of boredom. She studied the way his eyes shone when he talked about it, and she became speechless.

Sometimes she found him truly moving. *This guy is burning with genuine ardor*, she'd tell herself, *deep down he's fascinating*.

Literature was fascinating. He was nothing. He told her about the time when he believed he could become a writer, the mad hope he'd nourished until the painful realization that he wasn't one, that he didn't have the gift.

This type of conversation affected her. She found him unalterably handsome, unalterably gorgeous as he stood half-naked in the kitchen crushing some ice and smoking a cigarette, telling stories in the half-light. Worst of all was that, on top of it all, he was a great sexual partner, something she hadn't experienced for years.

"Sometimes they're so mediocre that—how can I explain it?—I feel ashamed," he confessed. "That I could be taken for such an imbecile. Expected to swallow such gibberish, stuff that's so poorly written. But where do they come from? Tell me. Where do they dig up such poverty? Listen, there are no more than a half dozen major living writers in this country—it isn't complicated. Don't ask me what the others are pretending to be, Myriam, because I really don't know."

*It was hot. A haze of heat still hovered above the lake at bed-*time. Myriam was smiling, but it was obvious to him that she was disappointed. Had he found a single one who hadn't asked for the same thing? Every hour, every minute, Myriam had seemed different than students he'd known, but suddenly she'd become part of the same mentality. Now it was becoming absolutely necessary to go to his place. Now the curiosity to see it was becoming too intense. None had resisted it. You could almost laugh about it. All he had to do was express a total lack of interest in their seeing his place, rendered even more deadly by his sister's exacting surveillance of his comings and goings as soon as night fell, and they began insisting more, pressuring him to give in.

Quite often, after finally saying they could come over, he ended the relationship the next day, unless the young woman deserved extra attention and would benefit from a reprieve that could last a month, or even a month and a half, like that athletic Australian who'd helped him master the hot keys on his word processing program, configure his mailbox, import images, bid higher on a leather Hatteras cap from Stetson that he'd never worn. He still sometimes got letters from that former young blonde, who'd ended up in Paris and was having children while waiting for something better, and who wrote him to say she was sorry about having sabotaged everything and trying to force her way into his life so stubbornly. Sure. But maybe she hadn't lost out on the deal, despite everything. Maybe having children was the key, he'd tell himself sometimes.

Maybe there was a risk that Myriam would end up coming on too strong. The moment he'd climbed behind the wheel of his car, the thought that she wasn't any different from the others had crossed his mind, but he'd quickly understood he was wrong. They'd barely left the city and entered the shade of the forest when he'd made up his mind: he was thrilled that she was there at his side, thrilled that he wasn't experiencing that uneasiness that poisoned his heart every time he brought a girl back to the house, that vague and confused feeling of guilt each time he tiptoed across the entranceway with his shoes in hand, a finger to his lips, so terrified at the idea of running into Marianne on the way that all his muscles ached.

When he rode with a passenger, the Fiat couldn't be counted on for the same performance and seemed to crawl along despite the fact that he pushed the accelerator to the floor. He kept it in second, sometimes shifting into third to give it a few moments of respite and ease up on the motor, which was roaring like an airplane engine pumping out propellant; but what difference did all that make in comparison to the wonderful time he was having with her, zigzagging through the drowsy woods, listening to Gershwin as interpreted by The Residents; what importance could it possibly have?

Of course, he had no intention of making it obvious they were here together in the house. He had no intention of doing such a thing any more than was necessary; but something amazing was happening. It was so obvious. He let go of his stick shift in favor of Myriam's thigh and turned toward her, smiling.

Since the Fiat was beginning to choke, for the time being

he traded his passenger's thrillingly warm and tender flesh for the hard Bakelite of the stick and shifted down just before the next turn, which threw her against him. And that is where she stayed—a captive, you would have said, of a devilishly clever magnet—her head on his shoulder.

In the course of his entire existence, had he ever met a single woman who knew how to listen? The answer was no. The answer was no, a thousand times no, any way you looked at it.

Until today, until he met Myriam. Who not only listened to him but encouraged him to share as many things with her as possible. Had he ever had this feeling of lightness he was experiencing as he opened up to her more and more? After such a thing, was it surprising that no student could now find favor in his sight?

Annie Eggbaum could stick out her chest, rub her fleshy crotch against the corner of his desk—when she wasn't putting her behind on it—or take advantage of the lessons he was giving her to expose her body to him in more detail. She could swim bare-breasted as he went over the ideas bigger-than-life or less-is-more that were still essential but seemed so little known and still less used that it was astounding, a wretched shame; but no matter what she did, he still had no desire for her.

The student period was now like a dead branch. She teased him about the subject as they were passing below the place where the pit was located, brought up those girls who couldn't have failed to find him to their taste during a screening for some select group in the multipurpose auditorium, or when he was explaining why the very good writers made bad screenplay writers, and vice versa, while he strolled among the tables.

How was it possible not to think of Barbara at that exact

moment, her body lying in darkness at the heart of that hollow mountain not far from here, practically at the bottom of the place where they now were? He nodded vaguely. "There haven't been that many," he denied. "There's a lot of exaggeration to those stories. It's almost a myth." As he was scrutinizing her reaction, she sent a charge through him by running her hand through his hair.

"Was there something between the two of you?" she asked quietly.

He froze for a quarter of a second. Then let out a long, desolate groan. "Of course not. Myriam, of course not. That poor Barbara? I even have a hard time remembering her first name. But she was my best student."

"She would speak to me about you."

"Positively, I hope."

"Her tone of voice would change."

"Did her voice break?"

She stared at him as the lights of the house came into view. "It wouldn't bother me," she said. "The opposite. I think it would make us closer."

He parked without answering, stopped the motor, then turned to her, and gathered her hands to cover them with kisses. Was that what it meant to be moved? Is that how it felt? At the same time, he had a terrible urge to smoke. He leaned forward to kiss her and only then noticed Richard Olso's car, which was almost completely hidden by the shadow of the shed.

*M*yriam thought it was still too early for him to move into her place, but this wasn't indicative of any kind of reservations on her part. He reassured her. He wasn't about to land in her house with a trunk and toiletry kit like some kind of low-rent bohemian. That wasn't something he could imagine. Nothing would have seemed less attractive. They deserved better. They kissed. They also had to take into account the possibility—minuscule, of course, but a possibility—that her husband would reappear one day, spit back out from the black hole of Afghanistan. It could happen, she would say. As far as the army was concerned, her husband wasn't dead but reported missing.

He understood perfectly well. Everything was clear. No need to fret; he understood the situation very well. There was no hurry. The important thing was that he'd be able to see her as much as he wanted—that's all that counted for him. It allowed him to stand the horrible mood dominating his house now; it was the most dreadful atmosphere in the long course of their being brother and sister.

It was so palpable that his migraines had come back after a slight improvement. Even this morning he'd finished his lesson leaning on his desk, overcome by a kind of vertigo. "Are you okay, Marc?" asked Annie Eggbaum, who'd taken advantage of his tottering by holding him up and pressing him against her at the same time. "I wonder what you'd do without me," she'd declared as she guided him toward a chair.

Actually, the reason was because he hadn't eaten anything for two days, in addition to being sexually spent and having to face his sister's aggressions. Annie undid his tie and unbuttoned his shirt collar, then fanned him with the notebook in which she took notes in hopes of pleasing him. "Feel better, Marc? Can I do anything for you?"

Every time she called him by his first name he nearly choked because of the intimacy she was imposing on him; but aware as he was of the girl's personality, this freedom she took didn't seem negotiable. No matter; she led him next to the cafeteria, which was nearly deserted during class hours, and went to get him a slice of lemon meringue pie, which he swallowed without argument, feeling fairly thankful.

"Tell me what you want," she said while he was bending over his orange juice, sipping it through a straw that he'd cleverly bent toward him and was holding between two fingers. He shook his head, stared into space—not far from a clump of blue hydrangeas that shimmered like a powdery cloud.

"First of all, who is that woman?" she went on.

"That woman has a name. She's Barbara's stepmother. You want to talk about Myriam. But what business is it of yours?"

"What's this thing you have for old women? What's it mean?"

"Old? Hah. She isn't old. Besides, killing yourself before you're sixty is a pure waste, in my opinion."

"I don't trust her. In the first place, how could you marry a serviceman? Or anybody wearing a uniform? Couldn't be a very good idea, don't you think?"

"God knows where life takes us, Annie. God knows what we harvest when all is said and done. You decide to choose what's easy, and suddenly everything gets complicated. We pass the better part of our existence paying for our mistakes, you know, and that's not something I made up. Every day brings proof of it."

"You sure are cheerful early in the morning."

"The problem has nothing to do with knowing whether I'm cheerful, Annie. Who, in all decency, can be cheerful these days, except for cynics and the well-to-do? Tell me."

He smoked a cigarette with her and recommended she read Sherwood Anderson and William Saroyan. Then things would get clearer bit by bit, until all the gloom was chased away.

"Don't change the subject," she said. "You want me to find out about her? My father can get someone to take care of it. It's easy."

"No thanks, Annie, really. Definitely not. I don't want to find out anything that way. I'm asking you to respect that, okay?"

He knew enough about Myriam and didn't need to know any more today. She filled all the requirements. She was the exact model of the woman he'd always dreamed about, without knowing it. At this point, there was no doubt about it.

"What do you want me to tell you? Imagine a hurricane. Think of those mutilated trees, smashed-open houses, devastated gardens that they show all the time these days; think of those earthquakes, rivers of fire, overflowing oceans, picture it, Annie, and you'll have a vague idea of the effect she has over me."

She shrugged. Got up, then went outside to join a group of people her age scattered on the steps. It wasn't the first time she'd ditched him there, refused to listen anymore to talk about the effect that somebody else had on him; and on top of all that, a woman who was close to fifty, some kind of grandmother or something.

He made a friendly gesture, smiled at her, through the thick window of the cafeteria that separated them, but she didn't respond. He made another series of gestures to thank her, but she lowered her head. He got up and took his tray to the self-service area. Got another slice of high-carb lemon meringue pie, because he was going to need fuel to last until evening.

He thought of the various events that had occurred while he got ready for his afternoon class. He'd been forced to sit down in front of Richard Olso and assure him everything was going fine and that he was perfectly capable of going back to work today, that he was giving his word, that it was just a simple vagus nerve problem that included a mild facial paralysis that transformed the slightest smile into a very unpleasant pout; and finally, he'd offered to sign a form holding the university blameless for any accident that might occur, which Richard made haste to accept and then immediately shoved into a drawer.

At that moment, it was only being acutely aware of what was at stake that had kept him from grabbing the poor devil by the throat.

He coughed into his fist. "By the way, Richard. I just thought. Let's see now. What are you planning to do with the equipment you set up at the house. Huh? Answer me."

"Oh? You're converted?"

He grimaced. "Listen, it doesn't really matter whether I'm

converted, Richard. I went to your brother's. I went over to your brother's store. I know the prices. You think we have the money to buy gear like that? I mean, come on, you take us for bankers, for god's sake. You think we're printing it ourselves?"

"Calm down, old man. Don't worry about the price."

"Don't worry about the price? Did I hear you right? Excuse me? I'm not supposed to worry about the price? And what about our old TV; what'd you do with that?"

He pushed open the door to class in a dark mood, raised his hand to call for silence, and planted himself in front of the windows with his hands clasped behind him. He was going to have trouble accepting this. More and more trouble. The slight shudder he felt in his neck came from all the eyes focused on him. "I want those who are worried—and I notice there are a lot of you—to know right now that my illness from this morning doesn't mean I've caught AIDS or bird flu or Creutzfeldt-Jakob syndrome. Keep your cool. Where's your spirit? We're not all going to die, friends. No need to get out your surgical masks."

There was this writer that everybody was talking about, obviously better than average, but his work was decked out with an appalling, wobbly, mannered style that was completely unbearable, whereas the critics unfailingly praised him to the skies and unanimously canonized him. He had stumbled upon one of his books when it was sticking out of one of the students' bags. Once he got hold of it, he paged through it. Skimmed a few lines, then tore one page out of it, and threw the book out the window.

It was always interesting to see where a train derailed, he told them, see what part of a sentence showed the weakness, arrogance, failure, provinciality of its author. On the blackboard he copied the first sentence that fell under his eyes and that had the gift of ending like the others—namely, in smithereens, a failed balancing act, a tourist trap, pure and simple. What incredible self-conceit you had to have to write that way, what blindness. And what lousy literature they were promoting from magazine to magazine—and what pathetic and ridiculous conventionality it was characteristic of, in this case.

He stepped back to admire his work, which ran along four lengths of the blackboard.

Sometimes, the battle seemed lost. Reaching the end of the year and finding this kind of literature among his students' possessions made his head spin, made him want to give it all up.

"Just take a look at this. Take a look at this hideous stuff," he said, shaking his head. "Where's Marguerite Duras when we need her, for pity's sake?"

Taking advantage of a break, he went out for a smoke in the hallway and ran into the detective, hanging around with the most innocent expression pasted on his face. It made him wonder why we pay such people when we're perfectly aware of their many comings and goings, cafeteria breaks, and croissant orgies as they page through a sports rag, not only in the morning, but at any hour of the day, not to mention their breaks on campus under the shadow of a nettle tree or linden tree, which really do look like siestas, etc.

One day the detective would be talking about an identity he needed to verify; on another, a student he needed to question; and on yet another, a stolen credit card; but wasn't it more likely that he enjoyed the company of young women, who were so numerous on campus—although he was married? What's more, they were half-dressed in this season and a perfect way to get an eyeful. Richard Olso had no particular information about the presence of a police officer on campus, unless it was undercover and he was nosing around collecting information on something no one knew about, a hidden trail, probably; but Olso wasn't against this extra security now that there were more and more shootings, which were encouraging adolescents to fire on others before knocking themselves off.

"You think she's alive? You don't believe somebody did her in?" chuckled Richard. "Old man, as far as I'm concerned, this cop can be walking around whenever he feels like it. I'm not interested in getting shot down by some little imbecile who's flipped his lid. Or by one of those psychos. Personally, I wonder whether we shouldn't be armed."

How was he going to be able to leave Marianne in Richard's hands? That was the only real question.

On the way back to his place that evening, after an exhausting day that had begun with a vagus nerve problem and ended with reading the work his students had handed in and that he didn't feel like dwelling on, he let out a long resigned sigh—class was ending soon, and in a little while he wouldn't need to talk to them about style, composition, language, elements he desired above all, although not a single one of them seemed to understand what he was saying. In any case, not a single one was capable of coming up with a true voice; not a single one had both enough restraint and enough daring to write three lines that were of any interest whatsoever. The level was low this year, yet again. Then what use did writing serve, unless it didn't, he thought, while the amber evening filtered through the dark woods.

Each year, he wondered if he was going to stop teaching—and he probably would have if it weren't for Marianne.

His walks deep into the woods led him more and more often to the conclusion that it was time to put an end to his academic career—he thought of himself as an impostor, paid to teach the unteachable—but he hadn't found the courage to chuck it all, to go live in a tree or inside a cave, because no student would have wanted to give herself to some hairy savage, and none of them would have followed him of their own accord, which was also food for thought. The sex had been an incredible revelation. The sex had allowed him to endure a lot of suffering, and he hadn't been able to imagine putting an end to it with any seriousness without his mind beginning to waver.

Taking advantage of the rather late hour and struck by some vague impulse, he made a stop before arriving at his destination. He parked the car set back from the road and climbed the path quickly and accurately, like a lynx, bent double and almost invisible—wheezing as he made his way and the pebbles rolled under his feet, twigs creaking and crackling. These sounds were familiar to him; he'd always heard them, sometimes mingled with his heartbeats, which became a lot louder when she was chasing him, during those terrible scenes in which she was hot on his heels and bellowing.

Less than twenty minutes later, he was creeping onto the rock that jutted out over the pit. He'd made it in good time, a good enough performance. If you didn't mind walking at a clip, it took a half hour, longer if you were carrying something. Twilight was ablaze. The surrounding forest pulsated with a profound silence, punctuated with drawn-out crowing from far away, sounding hesitant, rapidly swallowed.

However, he couldn't get his breath back. His chest was caught in a vise. Frantically, he brought a cigarette to his lips and turned onto his back. There was no other option for the pain. Very trying ordeals were waiting for him, in one way or another; unthinkable heartbreak was accelerating, swooping down on him, swirling around him. Not that he had never experienced turmoil, complications settling in, but not with such force, not so rapidly. He was gasping for breath—something that wasn't exactly the most practical thing for a smoker, but the taste of the tobacco in his mouth was enough to keep him alive.

He let himself slide along the wall while still capable of it. This time, no migraine had come to announce the crisis, no veil had fallen over his eyes. That wasn't a good sign, in his opinion. It was terrifying.

Without hesitating any longer, he inched along as best he could, tearing the skin on his back and chest as he moved between a sturdy root and a rock to keep from toppling into empty space; and there he hung with his eyes closed, neck pulled in between his shoulders.

When he came to, night had fallen—the silver disc of sky hovered about sixty feet above him. He was breathing normally. He was whole. He hadn't bitten his tongue. The moon and a few stars now, and everything seemed immobile. He felt better, the warning signs had passed. He was just a little damp, his jaw aching, his neck still a little stiff. Feeling more assured, calm; things had been sorted out. For a moment he pressed his cheek to the damp wall, thanking whoever or whatever it was that haunted this place.

He looked up toward the almost dazzling halo like a powdery cloud floating in the silent darkness and finally started to smile. He felt better. Impossible to explain how this bizarre practice he'd adopted reinvigorated him, how hiding for a while in the bowels of the earth seemed to restore him to life—a life that had improved, was now unclouded, leaving him ready to go on with confidence and determination, feeling more robust than ever. Impossible to know how the spell worked—it certainly was some kind of spell, a sort of magical, mysterious drug that he administered himself by finding refuge within those damp, dark, potent, overgrown, mossy walls that bristled like the gullet of a monster.

Bucked up. That's exactly what he was. He kept his smile for another moment before sliding a cigarette between his lips. He was shivering, his muddy clothing was soaked. But he didn't light up because now he had to begin his ascent and smoking cut off his legs and compressed his thoracic cage more every day. Not that the challenge proved particularly difficult—or out of reach for a man who'd done his training in the mountain infantry—but he wasn't twenty anymore and currently confused getting back to the open air and hoisting himself up and out with the idea of a rebirth. It deserved more than appearing with a cigarette hanging from his lips, in a volatile cloud of smoke that would be totally out of place.

He remembered a night when he was on ski patrol with a group of his comrades-in-arms and the person at the head of their column had fallen into a crevice. They put him on a stretcher and waited for the rescue squad. Someone had stuck a cigarette between the poor guy's lips; he gave up the ghost before finishing it, surrounded by a waning cloud of smoke—and had a fit of absolutely grotesque coughing. The incident had happened on a summer night, the year Saul Bellow won the Nobel Prize, and they hadn't seen any of the meteor shower that had been announced, been able to swallow anything at all, or smoke a single cig until daybreak—were only able to keep the filters clenched between their teeth like he was today, keep it in their mouths, and thank heaven for still being alive.

He plunged through a night that was now black as pitch, into the woods and back down toward the Fiat. Moving at a rapid, confident trot, without stumbling once—he'd had enough practice running among these trees, surfing among these bushes, elbows in, a cigarette cocked in his ear—and his breath returned.

Marianne was taking a bath. She examined him from head to toe with a suspicious look, but he raised a hand to reassure her, nodded as a way of confirming he'd taken the wrong road, that he hadn't been doing anything in particular.

She rubbed her neck and breasts with a soapy sponge. "I need somebody to look after me," she said in a dismal voice. She rinsed off.

As she was getting up, he held out a towel for her. That's when he made the staggering discovery that she no longer had a single hair on her crotch; it was as smooth as a bar of soap. She studied him as he tried to keep the gulping sound he made discreet.

M *yriam had little interest in Marianne's body hair, al-*
though she acknowledged that the removal wasn't an
insignificant detail. It was her opinion that he ought to be happy
about this sign of emancipation from him, interpret it as a glimmer of such a thing, the germ of a kind of disengagement that
could only benefit both of them.

Of course, nothing was as simple. Obviously, the strength
of his feelings for Myriam inclined him not to do or say anything that could endanger the incredible time he was having
with her, the unimaginable experience of living with a woman
for the first time in his life. He nodded. This was their first long
weekend together, and not a single blade of green grass was
missing from the countryside where they'd gone—after several
attempts at leaving, which had failed because of hesitation on
the part of one or the other—not a single petal was missing
from the acacias bordering the hotel, not one butterfly or ripple
of fresh air, etc.; and that's just the way he wanted it. He nodded again, admitted that she was right. He had to act positive.
They'd been in bed for thirty-six hours, and the only time their
feet touched ground was to go to the bathroom, toilet, bidet,
shower, bathtub, minibar, or window as night fell over the

gilded countryside, or again at noon for the blaze of light they'd been watching for between the gap in the curtains.

They were bushed. Still naked, he smoked a cigarette, leaning against the back of the bed, while she lay spread out among the sheets, her arms crossed, laughing and claiming—as if talking to herself—that she had to be dreaming, that she was out of her mind. Smiling, he stretched out a foot to touch her. He regretted not being a writer. She deserved one. In the middle of the night, he'd read her a short story by Charles D'Ambrosio, and although she claimed to know nothing about literature, he could tell she had sound taste and a reasonably good ear. She deserved better than him, at any rate.

Lighting a second cigarette with the first, in the hushed atmosphere of night, he thought again of his sister's sex, now smooth as the skin of an apricot or fine luxury leather, pale as a new almond, undeniably astounding, at any rate; and just the idea of Richard being able to slip his hand down there took a sharp swipe at him, literally leaving him stunned.

Myriam maintained that he mustn't become preoccupied with the choices his sister would make. She looked him straight in the eye. Since they'd taken the hotel room the other morning, in such lovely weather, she'd continually reminded him that his and Marianne's lives were now separate, finally on a path toward normality, doing what came naturally, returning to a world in which brothers did not live with their sisters as if they were almost husband and wife, and no matter how vehemently he disagreed about this point in particular, he sensed that he wasn't being very convincing.

With a kiss she pushed him back onto the bed and mounted him, and made him experience moments for which he would have almost—to put it one way—been willing to lay down his soul. She wriggled against him like a worm, squeezing her breasts; and as she did, he felt himself shooting into her like a skyrocket.

He raised the sound on his earphones to listen to Greg Brown's "Downtown" and bit his lip. Myriam had fallen into a doze against him, his arm around her, and there was nothing he could have wanted more. Not even being the writer that he hadn't been, a renouncement that gave him a certain sense of pride, considering what it meant to him. The intense emotions he felt for this deserted woman sleeping against his shoulder flabbergasted and confused him yet again.

Had he ever imagined such a thing could happen to him? He felt as if he'd been drugged, that the high had intensified as the hours and days went by.

The situation in Afghanistan was hardly settled, but she didn't seem worried about it. She studied him with a smile on her face, shaking her head and repeating that she was out of her mind. "How can I have a relationship with a man?! . . . ," she would exclaim from time to time, her face taking on a horrified look. "I'm married! . . . How did they manage to stuff so much madness into a brain as small as mine?"

"We can't abandon that country after having mucked it up so much, Myriam. We should have thought of that before. I'm talking about the troops we have over there. Once you've meddled with something, you've got to see it through, there's no other choice."

"I'm just trying to say that I had no idea things would turn out this way between us."

"I'll speak to him. If he comes back, I'll speak to him. But I don't really think he will. He hasn't given any sign of life in too long a time. Wait and see if somebody rings your doorbell, or wait to get bad news. And a medal, obviously."

"We certainly will. I'm not thinking about that. Let's not talk about him. Look at me. Was it you I was waiting for? Was it you I took so long to find?"

Moved, he rolled on top of her and took her in his arms. This first weekend they were spending together, two hours away by car on the opposite shore of the lake, was going to their heads. They were talking idiotically, gazing idiotically, into each other's eyes, floating on some kind of idiotic cloud that they weren't trying to get off.

A few days before, he'd had to face facts. Annie Eggbaum had taken advantage of a particularly balmy day to glue herself to him and whisper into his ear about the results of the research her father's henchmen had carried out. He was annoyed, but listened anyway—after asking her to take a step back and behave herself.

For a moment, that black veil had swooped down on him. The buildings on campus had started to twinkle, and the grass lit up, caught on fire like sulfur. Then he'd got hold of himself. Thanking Annie, he'd let her hang from his neck and rub against him for two or three minutes. "Let's forget it. Come over to my place and rest," she'd offered, full of hope.

"Tell me, Annie, is this about a bet? Did you make a bet?"

Such dedication, stubbornness. Obviously, these simple qualities would have deserved more consideration, attention; but he had no more time to devote to her now—ever since the first moment he'd laid eyes on Myriam, ever since he'd felt that electricity under his fingers when he touched her, ever since he'd felt the grip of her white thighs, had kneeled before her frothing wellspring, etc. He'd gone home and lay down.

His telephone had rung several times. Around twenty novice writers panicking, obviously, at the idea of failing one of his courses; or even Richard trying to reach him to find out what was happening. He stayed on his back for part of the afternoon, foundering in a half-sleep.

He'd brooded like this until evening, in the empty, silent house, gliding like a dark pebble into the bronze light of dusk. He stayed lying on his upstairs bed, which he'd furnished with a wonderfully comfortable mattress pad, knowing as he did how indispensable a good sleep was. Then he decided that he didn't regret anything. Decided that, as a whole, the balance sheet was in the black, that the price to pay had no importance. He'd sat up and grabbed his phone to reserve a double room in a quiet place.

He'd bought new sports shoes and had a strong desire to give them a try. Wanted to run through the woods a bit. Maybe toward the cave, he wasn't sure; he just needed to get out, breathe. The idea of going away for the weekend with her sparkled like something fallen from the sky, like a lantern being waved in the night, pointing the way to the house, the ultimate destination. Basically, everything was clear.

*T*he room was actually a cottage at a motel. He'd chosen the one that was the most out of the way and laid away a large stock of cigarettes.

Now he knew what sweetness was. He understood from now on what a woman had to offer, beyond sex. He had the hang of it. He felt at peace.

He pushed her away gently—she was slipping and tumbling off all the time—then he got up to look outside. The front fender of the Fiat was so damaged that it looked like it had run into a tree. They had hit a buck on their way there, which had come out of the woods while he was driving without concentrating, perhaps because he was still disturbed by the information Annie had given him a few days before. The animal had suddenly appeared against the sunlight, and they'd hit it head on.

The hotel management had sent a bottle of champagne to their room. They'd hurried to drink it before they'd even gotten their breath back. Nothing had happened to them, but the animal had taken quite a while to die. They'd undressed hastily and started their fabulous weekend without even taking the time to open their bags, in the spirit of the type of unbridled sex triggered by nearness to death. The animal had died just as they were deciding to pull it onto the shoulder, despite the fact that it weighed more than four hundred pounds, and its blood emptied onto the pavement in the most horrendous way, until the police arrived.

Thirty-six hours later, nothing about the view had changed except the light: the forests plunging toward the lake, the distant mountains, clear sky. Through the large window, he felt the mild air touching his bare skin, especially his testicles. Soon the lake would come alive in an ocean of fire, its banks coated with flames. He picked up his sunglasses.

The house had ended up burning, from cellar to attic. The upstairs had caved in with a grim roar. He'd stayed there another ten or so minutes without batting an eyelash—although he was far from being in good shape on the brink of his fourteenth birthday and was reeling a little, his cheeks still smarting, his eye swollen—then he turned on his heel. Nor did he faint until he'd gotten a little farther, to the edge of the path. First he fell onto his knees, then collapsed flat onto the tar road as Marianne came running, a few seconds too late to break the fall, her arms stretched out toward him, full of despairing, moaning adolescent sorrow.

He touched Myriam's foot to show her the squirrel that had come into the room, attracted by the smell of cold toast swollen with maple syrup. How could he blame her for anything? He studied her lying on pillows; she looked washed out, cold. He wondered if the fact that she was a police officer didn't sometimes add to her appeal.

In any case he had no intention of bringing up the subject with her. Of telling her that he knew, that she was unmasked. What was the use? Running over a buck was a bad sign. They'd seen themselves in its dulling eyes, and that wasn't good either, not a good omen; but even so, they'd kept the clouds at a distance. They'd had to. This was their first long time together, their first weekend alone.

He tried to imagine her in her navy-blue uniform. The day before they'd left, while she was sleeping, he'd ended up finding her weapon—hidden at the bottom of a boot under a thick wool sock—and had had the chance to examine it in the half-darkness. For a moment, he was stupefied by his incredible myopia all this time, despite all his famous rules, precautions. Often, in hindsight, you can only tremble at how close you came to the edge of the precipice without being aware of it, the risks you ran, the hair's breadth to which you owe still being alive. He shook his head. Opened the window to smoke.

Warm air flowed in. The noises around the motel pool became more audible, phone conversations, drinks, diving. For a moment, he almost suggested they go for a plunge, but he reneged immediately at the idea of having a conversation with some young actor in his cups or a drink with the wife of a soccer player or any other double for Paris Hilton. Anyone had it coming who took the risk of heading for the beach umbrellas, strolling among the deck chairs at martini time, and sitting down with the others facing west in observance of that pleasant tradition that required you *ooh* and *ahh* at the sunset the way you applauded the pilot of a 747 who landed his aircraft without incident. It was the kind of infantile behavior characteristic of the imbecility of any group.

For how many miles around them were hotels fully booked every weekend? How many candles, dinners by candlelight, and adulterers were there? He grinned at the image of him that suggested, one he certainly had to take on, although he was sure she'd have preferred going camping and dining on kebab.

Ground glass sparkled on the carpet in front of the chair upon which he'd folded his trousers. When the TV screen had shattered, it had let out a hollow, muffled sound and rained down on his head through the slot in the box he was carrying at arm's length between two cars.

He'd just smashed the fifty-inch flat-screen that he was bringing back to Richard's brother against the corner of a heavy, rather old sign with a metal frame that yesterday's heavy winds had twisted and bent above the sidewalk. At the same time, an incredible pain had radiated from his coccyx, then disappeared immediately as if by magic, leaving him stricken, paralyzed by the fear of a second unpredictable attack.

"But what the hell are you doing, old man?" sighed Yannick Olso, standing at the threshold of his store with his arms crossed. He was the owner of Olso Hi-Fi, which specialized in top-of-the-line equipment. "What the fuck are you doing, jeez?!"

His back had fallen out during a hundredth of a second, really caved in. There was nothing to do about it, unfortunately, no treatment to follow except to wait for nature to reach the end of its slow, meticulous mending work, to keep from forcing his luck in the meantime by lifting heavy things.

Leaving the box on the sidewalk, he dusted himself off, shook his hair. "You were supposed to send me somebody," he'd said, "and you didn't send anybody. So here's the result. Great savings, huh? Zero."

"Was supposed to do it, but that's not the point," the other went on, shaking his head and looking crushed. "But are you supposed to be so damned clumsy?"

"Okay. Sorry. You got a glass of water, I need to take a tablet."

His migraine had come back. Once inside, Yannick Olso went back behind his counter. "You wouldn't want to try out a video projector?" he asked. "Check out the video projector. Listen to me. I'm sure I have something that'll fit the bill."

"How about a drinking fountain and some cups? So I can swallow these lousy thingamajigs," he'd answered dully.

That was the reason why, forty-eight hours later, minute splinters of glass were sparkling on the carpet, in the amber light of the setting sun, in the gold of its nearly pink, low-angled rays; they'd obviously fallen from the cuffs of his pants or some other folds in the lining.

He caressed Myriam's leg, which now had straightened nearly completely; it had been waxed just before coming. The fact that even an ounce of the desire he felt for her hadn't worn off after thirty-six hours of complete intimacy didn't surprise him. Nor did the fact that he hadn't tried to get away—nothing could have been less strange. But he'd known girls who let themselves be screwed while chewing gum, smoking, or taking inventory of the books in his library as they twisted their necks to one side. In what way could Myriam be compared to them? In what ways were they playing at the same game? When she held him tight against her breast, with shortened, quivering breath, how could he have resisted her? Then what difference did it make whether she was a cop or a nun?

The carcass of the buck was lying on the flatbed of a pickup truck, and although he'd called the management to ask them to get that nasty thing out of the parking lot, it hadn't been moved—all they'd done was send them a second bottle of champagne. *What hard luck*, he thought again, looking at the animal whose blood had stained the back of the van, then dried, and blackened. He was standing at the balcony window where their bed had been placed, and had a fairly vertical view of the buck, whose eyes were open. He'd asked that it be covered with a tarp at least, but that idea seemed to have been forgotten a long time ago, and he wasn't thinking about complaining anymore. For no particular reason he accepted it. A mat of dried blood gleamed like lacquer around the muzzle of the animal. He wished he could go back in time and turn the wheel a second earlier. He got a cigarette. There was no movement in the parking lot. Only a few black birds that were impossible to identify wheeled above the horizon, and a few branches barely quivered in the balmy air.

Noticing how pale he was, Yannick Olso had invited him to sit down for a moment until he felt better. But his brain was still on boiling when he went home and parked behind Richard's Alfa Romeo. It was a miracle when the tablets got the better of his migraines—if he tripled or quadrupled the dose. But the only real remedy he knew, developed by experiment, consisted of lying flat with his head on Marianne's thighs and letting her take care of his forehead and temples; just placing her caring hands there was enough.

Richard's presence absolutely annulled such solutions.

Richard Olso. Not a single girl on campus managed to find something in him. Not a single woman would have thought of giving him a glance. Except one.

What had led Marianne to throw herself into his arms really didn't matter. Why did it matter what made a woman commit this kind of noxious absurdity? He didn't want to think about it anymore. He would have given his life a thousand times for Marianne, and he'd proved it; but this was the result. Gut-wrenching. Outside, the blue sky was being copper-plated red. *Absolutely appalling, even,* he said to himself. *What's wrong with her?*

He leaned over the gas cooker in the kitchenette to light a cigarette because his lighter wasn't handy. Raising his eyes to gaze down on the parking lot, he again wondered about the scene below; was that a cloud of busy flies over the dead animal, which was exposed to the sun and covered with a lot of blood, or was it the effect of those migraines that had been following one another recently like waves, creating black spots that he took for flies?

He wasn't sorry about having shaken her up. That was nothing, compared to what she'd done to him. The reasons didn't really matter.

He looked at Myriam and wondered if God had created women to make men suffer, especially when women fell into the over-forty category and had that look of being deeply delighted and full of steely resolve. Obviously, he held nothing against her, had nothing to blame her for, nothing at all, because he knew she hadn't lied to him about the essential things and hadn't put up with his embraces like a bitter pill to swallow, but had sought them out aggressively and developed a taste for them, which she had no intention of hiding; now he understood what she meant when she looked him in the eyes and confessed that she was damned.

Between yesterday morning when they'd arrived at the cottage, and now, as night was falling, he estimated they'd had sexual relations about a half-dozen times, and each time had left him speechless—even after he'd taken certain measures,

187

obviously indispensable, but nothing he'd felt glad about. Despite everything, this weekend idea was turning out to be a fantastic one, he told himself as he leaned forward to examine Myriam's backside, leaned over her for a glimpse of her depleted, astonishing, swollen mollusk.

For a moment he slid onto her, onto her back. Not to indulge in some sinister session of sodomy under cover of dusk—although an inevitable erection went into action at the contact of the two hemispheres and the still moist and sticky parting—but to gauge the feeling he had for her beyond the betrayals and lies, to measure its strength and draw the comfort he needed from it.

There was a small chance that Marianne would prevent things from going too far. She was probably going to rally and convince Richard to keep it all the way it was; but what would the future be like from now on? To which lonely place could he go to scream if he and Myriam separated—and could he still keep it from happening?

He hadn't been to the house since the other day, when he'd surprised them sitting on high kitchen stools and given in to a fit of rage that his migraine, which had gotten worse and worse since he'd left the brother's store, certainly hadn't helped contain. He'd spent the night at the edge of the road in the Fiat, smoking cigarette after cigarette—which actually fed the migraine that was literally crushing the bones of his skull while he peered into the surrounding forest wincing with pain and perplexity. An ambulance went by, and later, as the moon was rising, he saw the ghost of his mother drifting across the sky and into the clouds over the mountaintops.

He placed a few kisses on Myriam's lovely breasts when she

rolled over to him on her back, and he sucked the tips a little while his mind took off elsewhere and his eyes went blank. He caressed Myriam's thigh and thought of his sister and the trauma of their separation. He ordered drinks and club sandwiches. You could hear voices, the soft reverberation of a plunge into the pool, the trilling of splashes, laughter, a few hundred meters from where they were.

It was obvious that the story would never sort itself out. That he could never set foot in that house again—their place, as they had still called it a few days earlier. And that is just what she'd told him while he was walking through the garden toward his car, his teeth clenched with all his strength—to the sound of the sowish squeals coming from Richard after he'd been splashed on the butt and back in the middle of his shag with a pot of boiling water. The situation was not going to work out.

The look he and his sister had traded before he left the premises—"Get the fuck out of here!!" she'd spit at him in a strangled voice, "Out of my sight, you piece of shit!!"—were definitive, at least. He reckoned it would take years—maybe dozens—before she'd be willing not only to speak to him again but to let him get within less than a hundred yards.

He wasn't very young anymore. Thinking of long stretches of time in the future was beginning to make him shudder. For a moment he wondered if he shouldn't have poured gasoline on himself to tip the scales in his direction; in a similar frame of mind, he'd stuck a potato peeler into his thigh one morning, forcing his mother to make an emergency call instead of raising her hand against him—and his father to take off his belt to use as a tourniquet.

He'd written a short story using this material in the

mid-seventies, after thinking he'd felt a strange emotion while considering a series of words forming in his mind, asking only to be typed out with a beginning and an end; but it was a false alarm. He remembered his sister's stubborness in repeating over the years that she believed in him and his potential as a writer, just because he was good at Scrabble and sometimes tried his hand at writing a few miserable lines of text. Obviously he'd failed, but at least Marianne's blind confidence and absolute certainty that her brother had a special gift had helped him keep his head high and prevented him from being destroyed by that horrible and complete tragedy he finally unleashed one evening after concluding that his mother would end up killing him—for hadn't she thrown him to the bottom of the stairs leading to the cellar not too long before, and used a cane on him?

Sometimes, in winter, when he was walking through the woods and an icy wind began to blow, his bones began hurting again in certain places. They'd said he had three fractures, but there had been more, he just hadn't pointed them all out; for example, his nose had only started turning black and blue two days later.

He'd waited to see the flames springing from the roof before thinking about drawing back, before thinking about reacting. He was barely fourteen and was standing before a kind of gigantic, sparking pyre that throbbed like a jet engine. The sight of it paralyzed him, and he stayed so long that the white-hot chunks of wood began raining around him like a shower of meteorites. Then his feet got entangled, and he fell awkwardly on the way to the tar road, leaving behind the skin on his arms and legs and nearly half his face as heaven's will was accomplished in back of him, and flecks of fire spun in the burning air. He'd passed out before Marianne reached him. The first fireman who arrived knelt on the ground and held him against his shoulder, caressing his face and, with lips contorted by compassion, said, "Everything's okay, lit'l guy, oh my poor lit'l guy, everything's okay, oh my God."

He tried to forget that now Marianne hadn't a hair between her legs and that such a ministration wasn't meant for him; but forgetting wasn't easy, the image stuck to the back of his mind.

What was he supposed to do now? In less than twelve hours, it would be sunrise again, life would continue, and everything would again become intolerable. Monday morning had usually been the worst day of the week, even during normal times. Richard would begin spouting the list of new bookstore titles, the weekly delivery. If there was any trash among them, an author completely without interest, you could be sure Richard would start praising him, vaunting his majestic writing, dazzling style, rich language, etc.—you could count on it like clockwork. And then he'd have to teach a class and claim that literature could save lives or cure lepers or God knows what.

He imagined Richard's back covered with blisters and wondered if his academic career still had a future. This time, he was bound to get kicked out; Richard would point to the door, and there'd be nothing he could do about it.

It wasn't the best of times, in such an uncertain economy, to be losing your job. The banks were tough and full of tricks, and the treasury department had an iron fist. He finished his sandwich feeling a kind of anxiety. Then he stopped thinking about it.

Apparently, being in love wasn't enough. Or rather, being in love was no longer enough. The lettuce leaves had gone a bit soft, the toast a little cold. Of course it was pleasant to think you had a choice in life, but the truth was entirely the opposite, a lot less amusing.

He grazed her calf with his fingertips and told her it was clear he owed her the best moments of his life, that he hoped she'd be blessed for that, for this feeling she'd made him discover; he hoped that, because of him, the gift would be returned to her a thousandfold. The put-on she'd used to approach him didn't matter, all that malarkey about a husband disappearing in the mountains of Afghanistan; all of it seemed so incredibly minor compared with what he'd obtained.

He wondered if she'd invented it all herself, or if they'd helped her put together that story about a sergeant lost in the middle of a mountainous desert. No matter what, it was pretty disturbing to imagine somebody fighting for you, at that very moment, in you-didn't-know-exactly what corner of the world, having to imagine blood flowing, men getting their heads lopped off, women being raped.

Quite an actress he'd been dealing with. He chuckled to himself at the thought, actually appreciated the way she'd conned him, the sheer truth within the lie. He raised his glass in her direction and for the moment gave up claiming to himself with all his heart that he didn't mind being thrown into prison if it happened at her own adorable hands. Then he took his phone out of his pocket and began scrolling through some photos of them together, sitting against the back of the bed with the sheet pulled over their legs, looking like disheveled but contented messes. "Wow, they're good. I like 'em," he said. "Soon you won't even need a flash. They're coming out with something new every day." He examined them with tenderness, became worried by her wanness, the lack of color in her lips, her pale cheeks.

Annie Eggbaum called to see if he could give her a date, and he answered that all she had to do was name one, and it was hers, and Annie pricked up her ears for an instant, wondering about this new attitude of his. "They say a woman's mind keeps changing," he told her, "but we men are pretty much the same as you. We don't know any more about where we're headed than you do. At least we have that in common. All our U-turns. Our erring ways. Do you follow me, Annie?"

"My father's waving his hand at me. Wants me to give you his regards."

"Good, Annie. Message received."

"Listen, Marc. Can I tell you something?"

"Sure. Go ahead."

"It'll be great, you'll see. Try to be cool. I'm not going to ask you to marry me. Relax. The only danger is your getting to like it. I'm being honest with you."

She certainly did want to have an affair with him. She went after it endlessly, with a consistency you had to respect, as if somebody had cast a spell on her. The girl was priceless. No way was she going to let up. They seemed to be made that way, in that family. Not into giving up.

Any night of the following week was fine.

"Okay, let's say Wednesday. My period will be over."

"Wednesday's perfect."

"Marc, it's about time I saw you."

"We can just meet in my office. You'll help me grade papers or something like that. I'll bring the condoms."

"Don't fly off the handle so easily. Think of that poor Zuckerman character in the Roth novels, what he'd give to be in your place. Come back down to earth a little, from time to time."

"Those details about incontinence send shivers down my spine, I admit it, but have you noticed what a sharp eye that writer had, what a sure step, how pricked up his ears were? Have I ever put you on? Sometimes I think we should only read poetry. Have you taken a look at Frederick Seidel? Astounding, isn't he? Took your breath away, I bet."

He hung up. As dusk unrolled like a veil of purple velvet to the level of the fiery horizon, three men armed with sharpened knives ran out of the kitchens and charged straight to the pickup truck that held the buck.

Everything was dexterously completed in a few minutes. These guys knew what they were doing. Each of them went back inside with a nice piece under his arm, a haunch of venison, pounds of cutlets, meat to cook up at the best price there was. They'd left the head; propped against the slatted side of the truck, it seemed to have turned in his direction.

He went out for a second, long enough to cover it with a white robe from the motel; then went back inside.

He sat down again near Myriam. The choice had been so terrible, so difficult. Being in love wasn't enough; being in love was no longer the foremost consideration. Moved by his feelings for her, he took her hand and kept it pressed against his lips; he was upset, but he also felt helpless, incapable of fighting himself. If he was proving to be so stupid, then no one could do anything about it, no one could save anybody from that much ignorance.

Moments of liberation followed moments of anguish. He got up again. This time, the path clearly seemed more difficult to follow, a lot longer, a lot more dangerous. He walked to the stove and turned on the gas, pulled up a chair to the table, and sat down with his pencil and notebook. The gas was letting out a soft, sustained whistle. "Dear Marianne . . . ," he wrote, then stopped there and kept still for a long moment. Time felt suspended.

Suddenly, their ship had foundered. Suddenly, it was no longer a question of ending their days together nor of supporting each other until the end of time; it was no longer a question of anything. "Dear Marianne . . ." This wasn't easy.

He thought again about the brother he'd almost had and who would obviously have kept all this from happening—would have prevailed against their mother's brain. Outside in the parking lot, less than three hundred feet from him, the robe covering the animal's head made a vaguely gleaming spot in the darkness. Even if you weren't superstitious, you couldn't see it as a good omen. Running over a buck never brought any good. The opposite, in fact. Truly, the opposite.

Inside, the view was of him slipping a cigarette between his lips and reaching for his lighter.

Outside, the view became the cottage exploding like a lit-up pumpkin, splashing the surrounding area with its golden light.

Philippe Djian is the renowned author of more than twenty novels, including *Assassins, Frictions, Impuretés,* and the bestseller *37°2 le matin,* published in the United States as *Betty Blue* and adapted for film by Jean-Jacques Beineix. A #1 bestseller in France in 2009, *Unforgivable (Impardonnables)* received Le Prix Jean Freustié, a prize given to a French author for a work in prose. Djian lives in Paris.